Scary School Bus To Nowhere
Revenge Of The Goldfish

To Magdalena,
Hi!

Scary School Bus To Nowhere
Revenge Of The Goldfish

MM

JAMES LEE

Angsana Books
SINGAPORE · KUALA LUMPUR

Published by *A* *Angsana Books*

Angsana Books is an imprint of
FLAME OF THE FOREST Pte Ltd
Yishun Industrial Park A
Blk 1003, #02-432
Singapore 768745
Tel: 65-7532071, Fax: 65-7532407
Email: mrmidnightlee@yahoo.com

Cover illustration by Michael Lui
Cover by Mangosteen Designs

Printed in Singapore

ISBN 981-3056-35-5

A WORD FROM Mr Midnight

Ghostly greetings, dear readers…

Thank you for all your letters and ideas. They keep me awake at night in the graveyard.

I am sending a special prize to **Eugene Guo** of Rosyth School, who asked me to get him and his friends into trouble. Eugene, you are in *lots* of trouble when you step on board the SCARY SCHOOL BUS TO NOWHERE in this book.

Another special prize goes to **Bryan Lim** of Ngee Ann Primary School who sent in his terrifying idea about a goldfish that didn't have any bones. Bryan, you and your friend Tik Koon are in for some very fishy frights!

Meanwhile, all you other readers should send me your story ideas, too. If I use them in one of my books, you'll win a prize. Full details are in the back of this book.

And now, let's start getting scared…

Your frightfully good friend,

presents

SCARY SCHOOL BUS TO NOWHERE

1
MUM

So, you think "8" is a lucky number?

Hah!

And you think "888" is three times luckier?

Hah, hah, hah!

Have I got news for you. I'm Eugene Guo, and me and my friend Azizul Kamal Shah can tell you that "888" was not lucky for us. Why? Because "888" was the number of our school bus.

The scariest school bus in history!

Our terrifying tale began one morning when we ran down the stairs on our way to school. We were late, as usual, but Azizul was later than me. We could see our school bus heading towards us. But this big fat lady was blocking our path to the bus stop. If we missed our bus, my mum wouldn't let me watch TV for a week.

If only I'd known then what I know now. If only we had missed the bus. We could have saved ourselves so much *fear*, so much *terror*, so much — *danger*!

I jumped off the path and ran across the grass. It had rained overnight. With every step, my new sneakers sank further and further into the mud. Squelch, squelch, squelch. Soon they were a hideous yukky brown!

Azizul was smarter. He squeezed past the fat lady and ran along the path.

We just made it to the bus stop in time. The door swished open. We clambered inside, trying to catch our breath.

And that was when I noticed the *first* funny thing! The bus was empty. There was just the driver, Azizul and I. No one else was aboard. Where were all our friends? Lim Chee Siong? Mohamad Adib? Adam Teo? *Where were they...?*

"Azizul," I asked, "is today a holiday?"

"No," he shook his head, looking amazed at all the empty seats. "It's a school day."

As the bus moved off, we made our way to our usual place at the back. I looked over my shoulder. And that was when I noticed the *second* funny thing!

The driver was different. He wasn't the usual driver we had every day. *This* driver had curly, curly hair. It was coloured hair, too, like an orange. And his face was covered with little holes where he used to have pimples. And his nose looked sharp. Like an axe!

"The driver," I whispered to Azizul, "I know him. It's the killer."

10

Azizul turned white. "The k-k-killer?"

"Not a people-killer," I chided him, sitting down. "A chicken-killer. I've seen him. At the market. He chops the heads off the chickens!"

And just then, as the bus was driving along, that's when I noticed the *third* funny thing.

Only it wasn't funny.

It was scary.

WE WERE SOMEWHERE ELSE!

Azizul noticed it, too. He was shaking like a leaf, clutching his schoolbag to his chest like a shield.

"Hey, where are we? Something's wrong!" he called. "Look... where is everything?"

I was looking out the window already. We should have seen what we saw every day. All the flats and houses, the shopping centre, the bank on the corner, the post office, the market, the car park. Instead, NOTHING!

It was like we were driving through a mist.

Azizul was wide-eyed with fear. "I'm getting off!"

"You can't!" I grabbed his arm. "We'll be late for school!"

He looked at me scornfully. "What makes you think this bus is even going to our school?"

"Well, it must be going *somewhere*!" I snapped, trying to cover my nerves.

I rubbed the window with my hand. I thought maybe the aircon was fogging up the glass. But nothing happened! All I could see outside was this grey, swirling cloud.

"Are we still on the ground or flying?" I joked, not feeling at all funny.

Azizul was on his feet. "I want to get off! You can stay if you want to!"

"I don't want to," I mumbled, and started pressing the bell.

DING DONG... DING DONG... DING DONG...

But the red STOP sign didn't light up. Chicken-killer kept driving. There was just the back of his orange head and the grey mist at the front of the bus. Nothing else!

I could feel the cold tingles on my neck and arms.

"W-w-where is he taking us?" Azizul wanted to know.

"How would I know?" I gulped. Actually it was more like a *hulp*, half-way between a "Help" and a gulp.

"He's not going to stop!" Azizul wailed.

I rang the bell again. "He *has* to!" I said angrily.

DING DONG... DING DONG... DING DONG...

Nothing! The bus kept going. I choked back my terror.

"Maybe the bell isn't loud enough," I offered. "Maybe — maybe he's deaf. Maybe a chicken cut off *his* ear!" I joked again.

"Funn-neee," Azizul glared at me. "What are we going to do?"

I knew! "Jump off at the first red light," I suggested. "He has to stop at a red light, right?"

"WHAT lights???" Azizul screamed.

He was right! In all that grey mist, where were the traffic lights?

For that matter, where were the roads and streets and traffic?

It was like we had stepped out of our own world into *another* world, a grey world, with just me and Azizul and the chicken-killer.

Travelling on an empty bus to *nowhere...*

2
MUM

We kept going further and further. I opened my bag. I found my pager. I tried to switch it on. But it was dead. I tried again. It stayed dead. So we were cut off from contact with anybody else!

Azizul tried to open a window. Maybe we could just j-j-jump out? And land — *where*?

He unlatched the window, but it refused to move. Quickly we tried all the other windows at the back of the bus. Nothing! None of the windows would open. They were all locked, but *how*? Magic? No, of course not! No such thing, right?

"Can we break a window?" Azizul wondered.

"What with?" I shrugged. "I've got nothing sharp. And that glass is special. Safety glass or something. It doesn't break like normal glass…"

By that time, there was only one thing we *could* do. We started screaming, and yelling for help, and beating our fists on the windows. But the bus kept going. Chicken-killer didn't even turn around or anything.

So we decided to save our breath.

We slumped into our seats and looked at each other. Azizul was sweating. Sweating from his forehead, sweating down his cheeks, sweating along his upper lip. His eyes rolled around. Me? Well, I had this cold, hard lump stuck in my throat. It wouldn't go up and it wouldn't go down. My heart was hammering like a mad machine. And someone had let about a hundred icy cold butterflies go in my stomach!

I struggled to breathe. My voice sounded all squeezed.

"W-w-we've got to get out of here," I whispered.

"We have to think of s-s-something," Azizul agreed in a strangled voice. "But what…?" Sweat was even dripping off his nose.

"My dad has a friend in the army," I told him. "He's a commando."

"But he's not here now, is he?" Azizul groaned.

"No, but we could do what commandos would do," I suggested. I lowered my voice, just in case chicken-killer had microphones hidden under our seats. "We attack!"

Azizul looked even more scared. "Attack *who*?"

I pointed at chicken-killer and put a finger to my lips. "We grab him," I whispered, "and *force* him to stop."

"B-b-but he's bigger than us," Azizul protested, sweating even more.

"But there are *two* of us, and only *one* of him!"

15

"Y-y-yes, but —" Azizul looked at me as if I was crazy. Maybe I was. But it was better to do *something* than nothing, right?

So we lowered ourselves to the floor and crept forward down the aisle. The bus must have turned a corner in the mist. We were thrown against the opposite seats.

"Ow!" Azizul rubbed his shoulder.

"SHHHHH!" I commanded.

We inched our way forward, holding the seat legs to steady ourselves. I called a halt and looked up. Chicken-killer was still driving. So far, so good. He hadn't noticed a thing.

I gave the commando signal to advance. But this wasn't a war movie. *This was me and Azizul on school bus "888"!*

I was sweating, too. It stung my eyes. I tried to wipe them, but my hand was filthy black from the bus floor.

Soon we were crouched behind the driver's seat. Terror gripped me. My teeth started to chatter. I forced myself to show no fear. I looked at Azizul. Our eyes met. I started the countdown for our attack.

"Three... two... one..."

Together we leapt up and grabbed chicken-killer's arms. If we pinned him down, he'd *have* to hit the brakes.

And that was when Azizul screamed almost as loudly as me!

When I grabbed chicken-killer's arms, *they snapped off at the elbows*. I was holding his right hand in my hands. It was cold and stiff. I waved it around wildly and threw it away. And just when I thought I was going to faint, something else happened...

KLUNK!

Chicken-killer's head rolled off his neck, bounced off his shoulder, and landed on the floor between Azizul's feet.

"EUGEEEEEEENE!" he screamed.

He danced up and down, from one leg to the other, terrified.

"EUGEEEEEEENE! EUGEEEEEEENE!"

But chicken-killer's head was just lying there... LOOKING AT HIM! While the bus kept driving on, the steering wheel turning from left to right, right to left, ALL BY ITSELF!

3
MUM

I think I fainted first, then Azizul. Just the sight of
that headless chicken-killer and the bus driving itself blacked me out. The last thing I remembered
was chicken-killer's head on the floor, his blank
face and orange hair!

This was supposed to be our school bus, *right*? It
was meant to be just another ordinary, NORMAL
school day, *right*? But it wasn't! It was a nightmare,
freakish and hideous, trapped on a bus that had a
mind of its own.

My eyes closed, my knees wobbled, and my legs
just folded up.

THUMP!

I woke up, a minute or two later, shaking all
over. Then I *really* started to shake. Chicken-
killer's head was inches from my face, rocking a bit
with the motion of the bus.

Azizul was also coming round. He looked dazed
and his white school shirt was covered with grime
from the floor.

"H-h-have we got to school yet?" he croaked.

"I d-d-don't think so," I groaned. *Never had I wanted to see my school so much!*

We struggled to stand up, gripping the back of the driver's seat. The bus was still moving, but bumping a lot, as though we were on a rough road.

WE WERE!

As I hauled myself higher, the windscreen came into view. For a moment I couldn't believe my eyes. The swirling mist had cleared. All I could see was green! We were in the middle of a jungle, bouncing along some kind of deserted farm track between towering trees cloaked with vines. There was a sudden turn in the track. A scream leapt to my throat. At the last moment, the steering wheel spun and the bus took the corner easily.

I wiped the sweat from my forehead.

"I can't watch," I mumbled, but somehow my eyes remained glued to the road ahead.

And that was when I felt Azizul's hand on my shoulder. Squeezing my shoulder, then shaking it roughly.

"Eugene..." His voice was hollow. "T-t-turn around," he begged. "P-p-please turn around..."

He sounded so quiet, so fearful, I took a deep breath and turned slowly. What now, I wondered. What *else* could go wrong?

"Oh no..." I breathed.

THE BUS WASN'T EMPTY ANY MORE!

Now, you may think that would have cheered us

up. Like, we had someone to talk to. But, well, it wasn't *quite* like that.

Yes, all the seats *were* occupied.

BUT ALL BY THE SAME PERSON!

A short, fat little man, with a thick, black moustache and thick, black, oily-looking hair.

And he was wearing a bright orange shirt and blue shorts.

And there were fifty of him, of *them*, sitting in every seat!

"I want to go home!" wailed Azizul.

"We'll be home soon," said the fifty men who all looked the same.

"No-o-o!" I gasped, hanging on to Azizul.

Suddenly he stiffened.

"Eugene," he whispered, "I know that man..."

I was about to ask which one, but that would have sounded dumb. "W-w-who is he, are they?" I asked.

Azizul leaned closer. "I've seen him, them, before... lots of times... when I go to my uncle's market..." Azizul swallowed. "He's the man, the men, the man who sells the fish!"

"Huh?"

We looked at each other.

"Are you sure?" I demanded.

"The fish man," Azizul nodded.

I stared at the fifty fat men with the fifty black moustaches and fifty orange shirts and fifty blue shorts.

"But it doesn't make sense," I puzzled. "First, the driver. *I* knew him. Chicken-killer! Now, the passenger. *You* know him. Fish man! It's like... it's like..."

"It's like they're real," Azizul thought, "but *not* real!"

"People we've seen before," I suggested, "but people who aren't *really* here..."

"But how do we know that?" Azizul demanded. "Are we here and *they're* not? Or are they here and *we're* not?"

I pinched myself. "Trust me, we're here," I told him. "The big question is, *where* is *HERE*...?"

We had started off in a mist. Now we were in a jungle. So much had happened in such a short time. If only we'd missed this crazy bus!

We looked at the fifty fish men who all looked the same. And the fifty fish men all looked at us. Nobody said anything. Well, almost nobody...

"THIS BUS TERMINATES HERE!"

Azizul jumped. "Who said that?"

"I hate to tell you this..." I pointed to chicken-killer's head. "I-I-I think *it* did."

As we watched, chicken-killer's lips moved again.

"THIS BUS TERMINATES HERE!"

4
MOM

"HELP!" screamed Azizul, pushing past me and running to the back of the bus. I was right behind him.

We clung to the pole at the back, surrounded by the fish men.

"Dead heads don't t-t-talk," Azizul stammered.

"Th-th-that one does!" My fingers were so sweaty I almost lost my grip on the shiny pole. "We've got to get out of here!"

"But we're in the jungle," Azizul cried. "Where do we go?"

I shrugged. "Maybe we can find our way home… or maybe someone will find us…" I looked at the fish men. "Or maybe your fish man will go somewhere we can follow…"

"I don't want to follow him!" Azizul hesitated, staring at the nearest fish man. "M-m-maybe he's like your chicken-killer. I mean, m-m-maybe if we touched him, his head would fall off, too!"

I shot him a grin. "You want to try?"

Azizul looked like he'd rather see *my* head fall off. "It's not funny! We might never get to school…" He thought some more. "We might never even get *home* again…"

I put a sweaty, shaky arm around his shoulder. "I was only trying to cheer you up." I stared at the fish men, too. "But maybe you're right. Maybe they're dummies or something. Maybe they're not really the fish man."

"So *who* are they?" Azizul begged. "And what do they want with us?"

"Maybe it's not us," I suggested, "maybe it's someone *else* they're waiting for. Maybe we just happened to get onto the wrong bus."

But something inside told me I was wrong. We *were* on the right bus. We *were* meant to be on this bus. And we *were* meant to meet chicken-killer and fish man.

And that really scared me!

Because it meant Azizul and I were *targets*.

Somebody wanted us to be here. Somebody was trying to scare us. Somebody… but WHO?

And WHY…?

"Listen!" Azizul shook me.

I heard it, too. A weird, high-pitched whistling sound. Like an icy gale. The kind of noise the wind makes, blowing through a broken window at midnight.

And as the wind grew louder, the bus got slower.

"We're stopping!" Azizul looked around, wide

eyed. "But why here?"

I didn't tell Azizul, but I had a horrible feeling we were about to find out!

WOOOOOOOOOOOOOOOOOOO!

The wind was now deafening and we clapped our hands over our ears. The noise made my head spin.

The bus was still moving, turning off the farm track and along a narrow path through the jungle. Vines and branches slapped and scraped against the windows. The sunlight was blocked out by thick treetops. We were moving into a dark, gloomy world of weird shapes and shadows. And the wind grew even louder, howling all around us, but outside nothing stirred. *Everything was still!*

"Look!" Azizul pointed.

The path ended at a huge tree, draped with masses of evil-looking purple flowers. As we watched, one of the flowers opened and swallowed a fat butterfly.

"We're going to hit the tree!" I yelled.

We were heading straight towards it.

Closer and closer.

Until, at the last moment, part of the trunk swung up like a gigantic door and the bus drove inside. We were swallowed up by a black cavern.

The darkness closed in around us.

The bus had stopped.

Someone had turned off the engine.

And then, nothing. Just silence. Like a grave.

"Now what…?" gulped Azizul.

5
MUM

When the lights blazed on, we had to shield our eyes. A strange blue-coloured light, more dazzling than anything we had ever seen before. And with the light, came one shock after another!

The fifty fish men had vanished.

So had chicken-killer. And chicken-killer's head.

And so had the bus!

Azizul and I were standing in a completely black space, not really a room, just a space. We were flooded with the light. And we were *not* alone…

A man was standing away from us, staring at us, with a mocking smile on his face. He wasn't young, but he wasn't old. In fact, he didn't seem to have any age. And he was dressed totally in black. A black shirt, a black bow-tie, a long black coat, and black pants. He looked a bit like a magician.

"So at last we meet," he announced. "Eugene and Azizul, I hope you enjoyed your little trip."

Azizul was looking around, frowning. "Where's the… the… tree? Are we inside the tree?"

"Tree?" sneered the man in black. "*What* tree? You only *thought* you saw a tree."

"We did see it!" I was getting annoyed. "The bus drove inside it!"

"And who would ever believe you?" the man asked me. "Buses don't drive into trees, Eugene," he smirked. He took a step towards us. "Perhaps I should introduce myself. I am the Memory Man."

"The *what*...?" Azizul shook his head. "What are you? Some kind of... magician?"

"Magician?" The Memory Man's mouth turned down in disgust. "Tsk, tsk, tsk. How insulting. I am an *illusionist*," he declared proudly, "the best illusionist in the world."

"Like David Copperfield on TV?" I asked.

The Memory Man laughed. "My little friend, I am the master of *all* illusionists! I can make you think, and see, and do, anything I want!"

"L-l-like just now?" My head was spinning again. Whoever he was, the Memory Man was very, *very* dangerous.

"Exactly. When you are in my power," he smirked, "your mind becomes my toy."

"I don't believe you!" Azizul shuddered.

"My friend," said the Memory Man, "I can make you believe anything. And there's *nothing* you can do to stop me."

"H-h-how...?" My voice sounded very thin.

"Simple, simple, simple," the Memory Man told us. "My illusions are based on your memories. Your

26

memories of your school bus, your memories of other people you've seen before. If I can make you believe *one* thing is real, you'll believe *everything else* is real, too, no matter how incredible it is."

He snapped his fingers and a huge picture of a human brain seem to float in the darkness behind him.

"Your brain is full of memories. When I control your memories, I can control you," he explained. "Whatever I need is already in your mind. Memories of things, of places, of people. All I have to do is put them together in *different* ways."

"So when we saw our bus…" I began to say.

"It *looked* real. It looked just the same as you remembered it. And when you got on board, the driver was someone you remembered. So he became real for you. As did the fish seller. Because they were real in your memory, I could make them become real again in your life. So real, in fact, that you actually *believed* all those strange things were happening to you."

"B-b-but they didn't happen," Azizul wondered, "did they?"

"Of course not." The Memory Man lifted an eyebrow. "But now that they've become memories, I *could* make them happen again," he promised, with a very evil kind of smile.

"Don't bother," I pleaded. "But you haven't told us why you made all those things happen to *us*. You must have a reason."

"Such curiosity, Eugene," the Memory Man chided me. "After all, you are my guests."

Azizul frowned at him. "No, we're not. You've *kidnapped* us."

"But that would be a crime," mocked the Memory Man. "I've simply given you a little adventure, a sample of my talents, *before* we have our talk…"

There was something in his voice that made my blood freeze. "Talk…?" I asked him. Warning bells were ringing in my mind. *Don't trust this man!* I forced myself to sound really calm, really *cool*. "What do you want to talk to us about?"

The Memory Man shoved his hands in his pockets. He just stood there, rocking on his heels, regarding us like a scientist studying bugs in a glass jar.

"You see, my friends, I've chosen you for something rather special. Something you can do for me. You might even say we're all going to become… PARTNERS!"

6
MUM

Azizul and I, partners with the Memory Man? What kind of partners? It didn't make sense. We looked at each other, then back at the strange figure dressed all in black. That sinister smile flickered across his face again.

"You should be honoured," the Memory Man scolded us. "Now that you've seen how powerful I am, don't you think it would be a privilege to work with me?"

"But you *stole* our memories," I reminded him. "You scared us to death in that bus."

"So why should we *trust* you?" Azizul demanded.

"Well, if you won't trust me," the Memory Man gave a hollow laugh, "you'll just have to OBEY me!"

He snapped his fingers and suddenly a long, thick python was writhing on the ground in front of us.

I screamed and jumped back. The python unrolled itself lazily and stared at me.

Azizul grabbed my arm. "Eugene, it's not real! It's just another of his memory tricks!"

The Memory Man chuckled. "Is that so?" he asked. "Tell me, boys, have either of you ever seen a python?"

We shook our heads, frowning.

"Then it didn't come from your memories, did it?"

"So it must be... REAL?" I yelled.

It was Azizul's turn to scream. The snake's eyes blinked at him curiously. The ugly body unravelled itself further, edging towards him. Slowly its head lifted, higher and higher, and its savage jaws opened wider.

"The python is one of *my* memories," explained the Memory Man. "Would you like to find out how real it is?"

Azizul trembled, staring into the python's mouth. "N-n-no..."

"And do you promise to be more co-operative from now on?"

Azizul tried to speak. The snake had dragged itself even closer. Its massive tail was coiling up, ready for the final attack.

"Y-y-yes..."

The Memory Man snapped his fingers.

Within the instant, the writhing monster had disappeared without trace.

"I really don't want to punish you boys," he told

us, "but if you force me, I won't hesitate."

"But why *us*?" I asked him. "Why did you choose us? We can't do anything to help you."

"That's where you're wrong," the Memory Man corrected me. "Think for a moment, Eugene. Who are your neighbours?"

What a dumb question, I thought.

"Well, there's Mr Chow, and Mrs Wong," I began, trying to remember all their names and faces, "and then there's Mr Chong."

"Some more," the Memory Man prompted me.

"There's Mr Ramakrishnan, and Mr Ho," I said.

"Mr Ho…" The Memory Man held up his hand for me to stop. "You both know the Ho family quite well, isn't that so?"

We nodded uncertainly. I was beginning to wonder if the Memory Man was, well, wacky as well as dangerous. *So what if we knew Mr Ho?*

"And can you remember where Mr Ho works?" asked the Memory Man, his eyes mocking us.

Azizul scratched his head. "In a bank, I think."

"Good boy, Azizul. I can see our fun and games with the python have improved your attitude." The Memory Man rubbed his hands together. "Yes, your neighbour Mr Ho works in the local bank, the one that your school bus goes past every morning. Mr Ho, in fact, is the assistant manager of the bank, which means he has the *keys* to the bank."

"So what?" I asked, pretending not to understand.

"So because you are part of Mr Ho's memories, just as he is part of yours, I can control him," the Memory Man announced. "I can make him open the bank for me, whenever I want, and give me *all the money.*"

"No!" I shouted. "We're not going to help you rob a bank!"

But the Memory Man just smiled. "Eugene, when the time comes you will. And you won't even know you're doing it."

"It's not fair," yelled Azizul.

"Who cares?" the Memory Man shrugged.

"The police will get you!" I warned him.

The Memory Man roared with laughter. "How? It's all an *illusion*, so what can they do? None of it will be real, except for the fact that all the money will be missing!" The Memory Man fished an old-fashioned watch on a chain from his coat pocket. "Well, I've kept you long enough. It's time you were coming home from school…"

He snapped his fingers.

WOOOOOOOOOOOO… that eerie sound of a midnight wind howled around us. Suddenly a door flew open in one of the black walls. The Memory Man began to fade into darkness. Azizul and I ran for the door.

We leapt through it.

And straight onto the muddy grass near the bus stop.

Bus number 888 was pulling away. All our

friends were waving goodbye to us. We were on our way home from school, loaded with our schoolbags and homework, and everything that had happened hadn't happened at all.

OR HAD IT...?

7
MUM

Azizul sat in my room, gloomily staring at his homework. He called in every day after school and Mum always served us cool drinks and some treats.

"What's the matter with you two?" she had asked that day. "Such long faces..."

When we were alone, I sat up straight in my chair and tapped my pen on my desk nervously.

"It *must* have happened," I said. "I know we went to school. I can remember all the lessons. But I can *also* remember the Memory Man, and the bus, and chicken-killer."

Azizul wiped sweat from his forehead. "And the python." He looked at me anxiously. "Eugene, we can't help him rob a bank. It's crazy!" He shook his head. "Or am I going crazy, or what?"

"We have to tell somebody," I suggested.

"But who would believe us?" Azizul started pacing up and down. "If we tell the police, or our parents, they'll think we're nuts. They'll laugh at us.

They'll send us to a… a doctor, or something."

"What about Mr Ho?" I wondered. "Can we tell him?"

"But how?" Azizul shrugged. "What do we say? *Excuse me, Mr Ho, but your memory is going to be stolen and so is your money!* He'd tell our parents and then what would happen?"

I jumped up. "I've got it! We don't tell Mr Ho! We tell *Samantha!*"

Azizul stopped pacing. "His daughter! We see her every day at the bus stop! B-but," he hesitated, "do you think she'd believe us? Do you think she'd even listen to us?"

"It's worth a try," I told him.

But Azizul suddenly shook his head. "We can't!" He shivered. "What if the Memory Man finds out? What if he's — well, *watching* us somehow?"

"We have to risk it."

Immediately I felt better. Why should we let the Memory Man bluff us? Who did he think he was anyway? Maybe it had all happened in our imagination, the crazy ride on the bus, and the headless driver. Maybe our memories were just playing tricks on us. *Maybe the Memory Man did not even exist!*

Azizul agreed that we would talk to Samantha Ho the next morning, before the school bus arrived. That night, I set my alarm clock a little earlier, so I could be downstairs in time to catch her. Azizul said he was going to do the same.

I drifted into a strange sleep. I kept hearing an icy wind, and I was back on the school bus in the clouds again, and chicken-killer was wrestling with a huge python which ate his head. I woke up screaming, but nobody heard me. Then I was asleep again, and nothing disturbed me until the alarm clock jangled.

I met Azizul on the stairs. We hurried down and saw Samantha Ho, waiting with her friends by the bus stop. Suddenly we both felt nervous.

"We can't just tell her about the bank," Azizul whispered, looking at all the girls clustered around Samantha.

"Maybe we just say hello," I offered, "and we tell her we want to talk to her later… you know, after school or something."

Okay, so I'm chicken!

We shuffled closer. All the girls turned to watch us.

"Hi!" waved Samantha. She was our height, and quite pretty, I suppose. Like, she had long hair which was very shiny, and big eyes like the movie stars do. I mean, she wasn't exactly *ugly*!

"Hi," I mumbled. Azizul nudged me. "Er, Samantha," I began, "Azizul and I want to… er… well…"

"Yes?" she asked, curiously. All her stupid girlfriends burst out giggling. I could feel my face turning red.

"We've got something to tell you," I blurted.

"What is it?"

WOOOOOOOOOOOOOO...

It happened, just like that! That wind, that eerie, whistling wind, was blowing in from a graveyard. And suddenly, on the ground in front of us, with its jaws opened and its tail coiled up for the attack, was the python. And we could hear his voice, the Memory Man's voice, echoing again and again in our minds.

"I don't want to punish you... punish you... *punish you...* but if you force me, *I won't hesitate...*"

And his howling laugher was lost in the wind. Ice cold fear struck into the pits of our stomachs.

Azizul screamed. I screamed. And the girls burst out laughing.

"What's wrong with them?" one asked.

"Boys! Nerds! Stooo-pid!" said another.

We ran. Straight back down the path to the stairs. We collapsed onto the steps, trying to catch our breath, sweat pouring down our cheeks.

If ever I had any doubts, they were gone.

The Memory Man existed, oh yes. He was real.

And really powerful, too!

8
MUM

It was the worst day at school I'd ever had! I couldn't think. I couldn't answer any questions. I couldn't even remember what 2 plus 2 came to! I said I thought it was 5, and the whole class laughed at me. It was the same in every subject. All the things that I *knew* I knew, I *didn't* know any more. It was like all my memories had been stolen.

It was even worse for Azizul. When the teacher asked him where water came from, he said the tap.

The Memory Man was teaching us a lesson, I thought to myself with a grim smile.

That afternoon I went home alone. I sat in my room, staring at the wall, wondering what to do. I couldn't even remember what my homework was.

"Eugene…" It was Mum, looking around the door, with a very worried face. "You've got a visitor…"

For a horrible moment I thought it might be the Memory Man, come to my home to punish me. But he wouldn't bother, would he? All he had to do was torture me with memories!

I got up, following Mum into the lounge room. I guessed it was Azizul, feeling lonely.

"Hello, Eugene."

I almost jumped. There, on the couch, watching me with those big, big eyes was Samantha Ho. She was wearing a faded Boyzone T-shirt and trendy jeans. I mean, she *really* wasn't ugly at all!

I sat in a chair beside her and Mum served us biscuits and Coke. Samantha thanked her.

"My pleasure, dear. Eugene needs a bit of cheering up today," said Mum as she left. "He had such a terrible day at school…"

Samantha bit into a biscuit. "What happened?" she asked.

"I don't know," I mumbled, staring at my hands. "Just a bad day, I guess."

"Like this morning?" she asked sharply.

I shot her a quick look. She was watching me carefully. I didn't know what to say, so I just nodded.

"That's why I'm here," she explained. "I knew you were upset this morning. My friends shouldn't have laughed at you."

"It was nothing," I mumbled.

"Are you sure?" she pressed on. "You and Azizul were staring at the ground, like you could see something there, something really scary…" Her voice dropped to a whisper. *"Was it a python?"*

"Huh?" I leapt to my feet, almost knocking over

the snacks. My flesh crawled with cold fear. I was shaking with terror. "H-h-how do you know?"

Her eyes were different now, half-closed, studying me, as though she was trying to decide whether she could trust me. "And you heard something, too," she prompted.

"Like — a wind blowing," I confessed, "*howling*, really loud."

She nodded. "What did he call himself?" she asked in a very low voice.

I looked into her eyes. I could suddenly see how troubled she was.

"The Memory Man..." I barely breathed the words, so nobody could hear them except her. I fought to control my shock. "You mean, you've seen him, too?"

"I thought... I was going mad," she sobbed. "Crazy things were happening to me. People I'd seen before, coming back when I didn't expect them, doing silly things. Then this man, all in back, telling me I had to do whatever he told me..." She wiped away a tear. "I couldn't tell anybody."

I hate it when girls cry. Pretty girls are even worse. I never know what to do. I handed her a biscuit.

"What are we going to do?" she begged.

"Did he tell you why he was doing these things?"

She nodded. "Because of Dad. The bank..." She touched my hand, like it might help her. "I was even thinking of... running away," she swallowed.

"I thought, well, if I just ran away, *disappeared*, then the Memory Man couldn't find me…"

I was stunned. "Where could you go? Your parents would call the police. *Then* what would you tell them?"

"I was really scared. I knew what the Memory Man wanted, but there was nothing I could think of to stop him." Suddenly she smiled. "Then this morning, when I saw what happened to you and Azizul, I knew I wasn't alone…"

She kept looking at me as though she expected a miracle. What did she think *I* could do?

"Hey, don't worry," I told her. "We'll think of something. Three heads are better than one," I joked, my mind a complete blank.

She jumped up. "I knew you'd have the answer! *Wow!* That's really cool, Eugene!"

My mouth hung open. "It is?" *What had I said?*

"Think of all the memories we have! *We can share them!* We can put your memories into my mind, and my memories into yours!" she giggled. "Then the Memory Man won't know *whose* memories they are!"

I started laughing, too. "Really cool, huh?" Eugene Guo, I told myself, you're brilliant!

"Three heads against one Memory Man," I boasted. "We're sure to win!"

Hah! If only I'd known the truth!

I must have been crazy, thinking we could beat the Memory Man so easily!

41

We agreed to meet the next day after school, Samantha, Azizul and I. When she left, I went back to my bedroom and threw myself onto my bunk. I folded my hands behind my head and gazed up at the ceiling.

"Yes, what a real cool idea," I thought aloud.

It made sense, didn't it? If we all shared our memories, none of us would have anything to fear from the Memory Man. If he tried to scare *me* with a headless chicken-killer, Samantha and Azizul could tell me it was only a memory and not a real headless chicken-killer.

Brilliant!

I was so busy thinking how clever I was, I didn't hear it at first. A strange whistling noise, growing closer and louder. Suddenly a deafening roar filled my room. I was trapped in a raging windstorm.

Before I could do anything, a giant green python fell from nowhere and coiled itself around my chair. Its evil head lifted towards my desk and examined my homework. Somewhere, in the sounds of the howling wind, I could hear the Memory Man laughing and laughing.

I forced down a scream and backed away to my door.

"Hey, Eugene," a voice said inside me, "didn't you just say how brilliant you were?" I could hear myself mocking myself, and it made me angry. *It was the truth!* Where was all my cleverness now? Where was all that Big Talk? I was chicken! There I was, staring at the hideous python, scared stiff, shaking like a leaf, and the Memory Man had won again!

No, I decided. *No, no, no, no, no!* This time I'd fight back. This time I'd beat him. But how?

The Memory Man had boasted that the python was one of his memories. By making it appear inside that weird tree, he had made it become one of mine. So this morning at the bus stop, it was easy for him to make it real again.

Now, he was doing it again. Just like turning on a tap. Make Eugene think there was a python on his chair and he'd become a pathetic, pitiful idiot.

Okay, so think!

Think!

What could defeat the memory of something terrifying?

Easy! The memory of something happy!

So quickly I searched my memory. What could I remember that was really happy, really fantastic?

43

Got it! I remembered Samantha sitting on the couch, telling me how clever I was. *That was a very nice memory!*

I shut my eyes and thought hard, really hard. The picture of Samantha returned to my mind. There she was, sitting in her Boyzone T-shirt and jeans, chewing on a biscuit. The picture of Samantha got bigger and clearer. It filled my mind. Nothing else. Just Samantha.

Slowly I opened my eyes, then both eyes.

I couldn't believe it.

The python had gone!

Instead, Samantha was in my chair.

Well, sort of…

She was wrapped around it *like a snake*, a snake in a Boyzone T-shirt, a biscuit in her mouth, her head waving over my homework.

Oooops!

I shut my eyes again. Tighter. I concentrated even harder. I tried to remember how she moved, the way she talked, the way her eyes looked.

Next time I opened my eyes, she was sitting in the chair, nibbling a biscuit, smiling at me, and the whistling sound had gone.

It worked!

Wow, I yelled. WOW!

I could hardly wait until I met Samantha and Azizul the next day…

10
MM

When our school bus reached the bus stop, Samantha was already waiting for us. Azizul and I waved goodbye to our friends and jumped down. Samantha suggested we walk through to the small park behind our estate and talk there.

"Do you think the Memory Man is following us?" Azizul looked around.

"I don't know," I admitted. But we decided to split up, in case he was watching.

Ten minutes later we were sitting in the shade, and I described what had happened to me the night before.

"Does that mean we can beat the Memory Man?" Azizul asked hopefully.

"If I can do it once," I boasted, "why can't I do it again?"

"And the snake looked like me?" Samantha looked insulted.

"Only the first time." I blushed. "Then it was you!"

"How are we going to share our memories?" Azizul wanted to know.

"Talk about them, I guess," said Samantha. She started to tell us how the Memory Man played tricks with her memories. "The first time," she remembered, "I was shopping for Mum. I went into the same supermarket we always go to, but it was weird. It was almost empty. Just these strange people, people I'd seen before like the man who fixes Dad's car, and the old lady who does the ironing at the laundry. But they were different, their hair was funny, the wrong colour, and they did strange things. And then I forgot what I had to buy, and I bought all the wrong things, and when I took the trolley to the check-out, it had a python in it..."

"Yuk!" Azizul shivered.

"We've got to have a plan!" I told them. "We have to be ready for the Memory Man, *so he can't catch us by surprise.*"

"But even if we share our memories, what happens if we aren't together?" Azizul frowned. "What if we can't talk to each other?"

"Every time something weird happens," I said, "think of a *different* memory."

"So if I saw chicken-killer," Azizul grinned, "I should think of someone else, right? Try to remember someone else, with a happy memory. Like going to my uncle's house and eating all that good food... like *rendang*, like *soto ayam*," Azizul savoured the memory.

"But we have to be careful," I warned them. "We shouldn't talk about this any more. We never know when the Memory Man might be listening to us. We mustn't let him find out what we're doing!"

"TOO LATE…!"

I froze.

It was the Memory Man's voice.

But it was impossible! I looked around. *We were alone.* Just the three of us. Samantha, Azizul and I!

"H-h-h-he's here," gasped Azizul, fearfully clutching my arm.

"YES… I'M HERE… AND I KNOW YOUR LITTLE SECRET…!"

Azizul leapt up. His eyes were wide with horror. I was on my feet, too. *But there was nobody else in the park.* Just us three!

"Samantha," I asked, "you heard him, didn't you?"

But she was just staring at us, with a strange kind of smile, an eerie look on her face. My spine tingled!

And that was when we heard the high whistling sound, the wind howling from the tombs, circling around us, louder and louder.

And as we watched, Samantha Ho began to change…

Slowly, slowly…

Her face fading away…

Her body vanishing…

Like she was being swallowed up by a ghost…

Until it was the Memory Man sitting in front of us, his evil laugher ringing in our ears.

"You stupid boys!" he accused us, "you thought you could fool *me*, the Memory Man?"

"B-b-but where's Samantha?" I begged.

"You only *thought* she was here," he sneered. "You were talking to your *memory* of Samantha…" His voice became icy, his eyes glittering with menace. "I knew you were up to no good. I had to find out what trouble you were going to cause me…"

Azizul screamed. I screamed. We grabbed our bags and ran, the wind howling at our heels, and the Memory Man's cruel laughter echoing all around the park.

We sped down the path, rushed around the corner of the apartment block and crashed into a familiar figure. OOOOOFF! We went sprawling onto the ground.

"Hey, Eugene… Azizul, too… what's the big hurry?" Mr Ho asked us with a puzzled grin.

We just gaped at him.

"B-b-but what are *you* d-d-doing here?" I stammered weakly.

He looked very surprised. "I'm just going home early. Samantha isn't feeling well, so I'm going to drive her to the doctor's…"

But Azizul scrambled up, clutching his bag like a weapon. "You're not real! *You aren't really here at all!*" he yelled and raced for the stairs.

"Don't leave me!" I shouted and tore after him.

I glanced back once.

Mr Ho was standing there, a very worried look on his face. But whether he was real or not, I didn't want to find out. I could still hear that evil wind, rushing across the park, and the Memory Man's laughter was the most horrible, mocking sound I had ever heard...

11
MUM

I must have fallen asleep. Mum shook me awake anxiously, moving all my school books off the bed.

"What time is it?" I mumbled wearily.

"Time for dinner," she said, fussing with my homework. "You've been sleeping since you got back from school."

I sat up with a start. My window was still open, but now it was dark outside. The lights were on in the apartment block opposite. Suddenly I trembled. *I had a flash of memory.* Going to the park. Samantha turning into the Memory Man!

"Eugene, you've been acting very oddly," Mum began, looking at me closely. "Is there something worrying you?"

"N-n-no..." I shut my eyes. "Just tired, that's all."

"Mr Ho rang me tonight," Mum announced, then waited before she went on. I stiffened, dreading what he might have told her. "He said he saw you and Azizul downstairs this afternoon."

I couldn't think of anything to say.

"He said you both looked very frightened of something," Mum told me, waiting for me to explain.

"We saw this... this strange man," I admitted. *Well, it was the truth, wasn't it?* "So we ran away!"

"And where was he?" Mum frowned.

"In the park." I forced a smile. "But it's okay, Mum, he didn't follow us."

"If you see him again, I'll call the police," Mum promised.

"Thanks, Mum," I said, wishing it was all that easy. If only Mum *could* ring the police, if only the Memory Man *could* be locked up!

Mum looked back from the door. "Mr Ho said that Samantha had a fever. Would you like to take her some cakes tomorrow after school?"

"No!" I almost shouted. I don't think I wanted to see Samantha again, for a long time. Then I noticed how shocked Mum was.

"I thought you liked Samantha?" she asked.

I shrugged. "Well, she's okay, I suppose, for a girl."

Mum shook her head and left. I fell back against the pillows. I really *did* want to see Samantha. I had so many questions to ask her. Like, what had happened to her that afternoon?

Then I began to sweat. I wondered if her fever had been caused by the Memory Man? Was *he* the one who had made her sick? Was her fever something to do with his plan to rob the bank? I shivered.

I didn't eat very much that night. Dad asked me what the matter was, so I said I had a lot of homework.

How I wished I could have told him the truth! How I wanted to ask him for help! But I didn't dare. I knew that somehow the Memory Man was able to watch me, every single moment. He seemed to know everything I said, everything I thought. *I wasn't safe anywhere!*

Back in my room, I opened my homework and just stared at it. None of it seemed important. What could Maths do to help me now? What use was Science? And who cared how to change a sentence from the present tense to the future tense? *I didn't have a future!* I just had memories that the Memory Man played with!

I went to bed early. I pulled back my sheets and screamed. There was a python curled up, watching me, and I heard a sudden rush of whistling wind.

My door flew open and Dad rushed in. I must have turned very pale because he took one look at me and stopped.

"What's the matter, Eugene?" he asked quietly.

I just pointed at my bed. *What could I say?*

I saw Dad's face change. He suddenly had a very puzzled look. I turned towards the bed and gasped. The python had gone. The sheets were completely bare.

He patted me on the head and told me to get some rest. He must have thought I was studying too hard. Mum came in, too, and told me not to worry about anything.

I slid into bed, imagining I could feel the warmth of the huge snake on my sheets. Pythons must be warm, right? Or maybe they're cold? I didn't want to know. I just wanted to close my eyes and sleep… and sleep… and sleep…

Then I thought I heard that howling wind, as cold as the grave. But it was just my alarm clock. I slammed my fist down on it and lurched out of bed. I rubbed my eyes. It seemed so early. I hurried to get dressed, thinking up excuses why I hadn't done my homework. It was the python, it had swallowed my Maths.

Mum and Dad were still asleep when I dragged myself to the front door. My schoolbag felt like it was loaded with bricks. Downstairs, Azizul was waiting for me, red-eyed and half asleep.

"Why is it still so dark?" he grumbled. "Where is everyone?"

"Maybe they're all sleeping in," I mumbled back.

The street lights were still on as we walked to the bus stop. It was deserted. But our bus was already there, waiting for us, its headlights on, its windows in darkness.

"It's empty!" warned Azizul. "It's not our bus."

But it was. I checked the number. "888"… three

times *un*lucky!

"M-m-maybe we shouldn't get on," Azizul whispered.

We had no choice. A gust of wind raced around us, almost pushing us across to the bus. We clambered aboard and the door hissed shut. The bus pulled out into the street.

"Eugene!" Azizul's voice was choked with alarm. "Look!" He pointed to the man behind the wheel, the man with the orange hair and the lumpy face.

"Chicken-killer!" I gasped.

"And he's put his head back on!" gulped Azizul.

Chicken-killer turned to greet us. "You cannot stand while the bus is moving," he snapped. "It is very dangerous! You must sit down!"

I stared at him. He glared back. This time, it was the *real* chicken-killer. I was sure of it! So that meant chicken-killer was working for the Memory Man.

Azizul raced towards the back of the bus. I followed, past all the dark and shadowy seats. Suddenly I realised we weren't the only passengers. Two people were sitting in the back row. One was the fish man, a stupid kind of grin on his face. And beside him was —

"Samantha!" I yelled. "What are you doing here?"

"Samantha!" Azizul called. Then he froze. "Are you — *really* Samantha?"

She looked at him blankly. "Of course I am," she

replied weakly. Her eyes had a feverish light. Her skin was very pale. But she still looked very pretty, for a girl, with a fever.

"Samantha," I cut in. I leaned closer, dropping my voice to a whisper. "H-h-have you seen... *him*?"

"Do you mean me?" asked the Memory Man softly, suddenly appearing on the seat next to her.

The Memory Man had trapped us again!

And something told me that this time it wasn't going to be a game.

This time it was going to be for real!

He was going to unleash all his powers and make us partners in his crazy scheme...

12

The Memory Man looked from me to Samantha, and then to Azizul. He was gloating, patting his bow-tie proudly.

"Well, well," he chuckled, "we meet again. But this time it won't be such a long ride," he sneered at Azizul, "no jungle, no trees..." He looked out the window. "In fact, my little friends, we have almost reached our destination..."

The bus was turning into a narrow laneway beside the bank. Chicken-killer cut the engine and switched off the headlights. For a moment, nobody moved. We just sat there in silence. I could hear my heart thumping. We were going to rob the bank, *and it was too late to warn anyone*!

The fish man looked at his watch. "Four a.m., boss," he grinned. "Dead on time."

Somehow the Memory Man had cheated with our memories of waking up for school. *Four a.m.!* No wonder it was so dark and all the streets were empty. Our parents would still be asleep. No one would even know we were missing. I wondered what he would do next…

"Of course, Aloysius," the Memory Man nodded vainly to the fish man, "all my plans run precisely on time!"

I looked at the fish man. *Aloysius!* What a nutty name! I'd tell the police about him. There couldn't be many fish sellers called *Aloysius* for them to look for. Then I swallowed. What made me think we'd ever be able to call the police? The Memory Man might make us just… *disappear*… along with the money!

"All we need now is Samantha's father," the Memory Man continued, pulling a handphone from inside his coat. "Let's invite Mr Ho to join us, shall we?"

"No!" screamed Samantha. "You can't! Dad will *never* help you!"

"But he will help *you*, my dear, if he thinks you're in danger!" The Memory Man dialled a number and handed me the phone. "No tricks, Eugene. Just tell Mr Ho you're here at the bank with Samantha…"

My hand was shaking as I took the phone. I pressed it to my ear. I could hear it ringing and ringing. And then a voice answered.

"Hello…?" It was Mr Ho, sounding very sleepy.

"Er…" I hesitated, but the Memory Man nudged me impatiently. "I —"

"Who *is* that?" Mr Ho's voice demanded, starting to sound angry.

"Mr Ho," I began, my teeth chattering with fear, "this is Eugene Guo... it's v-v-very urgent, otherwise I wouldn't ring you so early... it's... it's about S-S-Samantha..."

"*Samantha?*" Mr Ho was really puzzled. "She's asleep."

"N-n-no," I told him, "she's here with us."

I heard the phone rattle. He must have dropped it and ran to look for her. A minute later he was back. "Where is she? Eugene, tell me!"

Sweat was pouring down my cheeks. "She's here with me and Azizul, at your b-b-bank."

He started shouting questions. "Why? How did she get there? Is she all right? What's going on?"

The Memory Man whispered into my ear. "Tell him to get down here fast! Just say Samantha doesn't look very well and wants to see him!"

I took a deep breath and did what I was told. "Please, Mr Ho, come down now, quickly! She wants to talk to you!"

"Tell him to come *alone!*" hissed the Memory Man.

I gulped for air. "She said, she only wants to see you!"

The Memory Man snatched the phone away and switched it off. He glanced at his big pocket watch. "He'll be here in about five minutes. Not a moment to lose!" He and the fish man stood up. "Aloysius and I have to make your father welcome, Samantha. We won't be far away, so don't try any tricks," he snarled. "I'll leave Albert to keep you company…"

So, chicken-killer had a name, too. *Albert!* As the Memory Man and Aloysius hurried from the bus and disappeared into the darkness, Albert got up from his seat. He was carrying a long stick. He whacked it loudly on one of the seats.

"You won't give me any trouble now, will you?" he laughed.

My mind was racing. Samantha was sobbing. Azizul was gaping at chicken-killer. *I had to do something.* Anything. But what…? Then I remembered. *Memories!* I could use memories, couldn't I? I could play the same tricks as the Memory Man!

I was trembling with terror. I looked around. I had to find something I could use. Aha! I spotted the strap of my schoolbag.

It was all I had! It would have to do! I pushed my bag down onto the floor, so chicken-killer Albert couldn't see what I was doing. I pressed down on the bag with my feet, and pulled on the strap as hard as I could. Nothing happened! I tightened my grip on the strap, pushed down even harder on the bag, and tugged with all my might. There was a sharp snap, and the strap broke loose from my bag.

Samantha was watching me, tears rolling down her face. She must have thought I was crazy, wrecking my schoolbag. Hey, maybe I *was* crazy, but I didn't have time to think about it. I just had to do whatever I could! I had to save Mr Ho and the bank!

I started winding the strap into a ball, round and round, and I stared at it, concentrating with all my mind. I kept staring and staring, until my memories of the python got stronger and stronger, until the strap was no longer a piece of green plastic, *but a long, skinny green python!* Its skin rubbed against my flesh, and I could imagine its jaws opening, ready to bite into my hand.

If I could believe it was a python, I could make Albert believe it, too!

"Alb-b-bert..." I called, with real fear in my voice, "d-d-do you like snakes...?"

13
MUM

Albert was half-way down the aisle, waving the long stick at us. His eyes popped wide with alarm.

"*S-s-snakes?*" He sounded terrified. "W-w-where have you got snakes?" he stammered.

"Right here!" I yelled and hurled the green plastic strap into the air.

"AIYEEEEEEEEEE!" he bellowed.

Samantha screamed. Azizul ducked. The strap flew across the bus towards Albert. For a moment I could believe it was a real, living, writhing baby python.

"PYTHONNNNNNNNNN!" he howled, dropping the stick and charging out through the door. The last we saw of him was a patch of orange hair vanishing into the night.

"Wow!" Azizul's eyes were as round as saucers. "Where did you get the python?"

"Eugene made it," Samantha giggled, "from memory!" She reached over and kissed my cheek.

Girls! Why do they always want to be romantic?

I just hoped that Azizul couldn't see me blushing as I leapt down the aisle towards the door.

"Come on!" I called. "We've got to stop your Dad before the Memory Man gets him!"

We tumbled out of the bus. I led the way around to the front of the bank. We moved quietly, keeping in the shadows. As we reached the corner, we could hear voices. Samantha clutched my arm. One of them was her father's.

"Who *are* you?" he was saying. "Where's Eugene? And where's my daughter?"

We edged closer, and I looked around the corner. The Memory Man and Aloysius were standing at the door to the bank. Mr Ho was holding a bunch of keys.

"If you want to see them again, you'll open that door and get us the money," the Memory Man told him.

"What are we going to do?" whispered Samantha.

Why do girls expect us boys to have all the ideas? My mind had gone blank. All I could think was how powerful the Memory Man was. And how big and dangerous Aloysius looked.

"You'll pay for this," Mr Ho warned them, holding out the keys.

I didn't know what to do! So I took a huge breath, and then ran towards him as fast as I could. For a second or two, nothing happened. Nobody heard me. Then suddenly the Memory Man spun around. He looked stunned.

"It's that stupid boy!" he screamed. "Stop him, Aloysius!"

Too late!

I snatched the keys from Mr Ho and raced back to the bus. I could hear Aloysius running and puffing behind me. I could hear the Memory Man yelling my name. I could hear Mr Ho shouting, too, something about the police.

"Quick! Back to the bus!" I called to Samantha and Azizul.

We jumped on board and I pulled the lever I'd seen the driver use. The door hissed shut behind us.

I was trying to catch my breath. I shoved the keys into my pocket and tried to think. The controls looked so different from Dad's car. I flung myself into the driver's seat. I saw this big handle near the floor. Was it the handbrake? I pushed it down. The bus began to move.

There was a hammering sound from the door. Samantha and Azizul were screaming. I glanced up. I saw the Memory Man and Aloysius outside, slamming their fists against the glass.

The bus was rolling faster and faster. I tried to steer it. But it was going backwards, down the alley, out into the street. Then it bounced against a light pole and stopped. So much for our escape. *We were trapped.*

"What would they do in the movies?" asked Azizul, looking around desperately.

"They'd make a lot of noise!" suggested Samantha. "And turn on all the lights!"

Good! *Except how?*

I pressed down hard on the middle of the steering wheel. The horn was deafening. So I kept horning, while Azizul and Samantha screamed and banged on the windows.

I started flicking switches.

The headlights came on.

Then the hazard lights.

Then all the lights inside the bus.

"Why doesn't somebody hear us?" Samantha wailed.

I began horning even harder. Then I had an idea. *The "SOS" emergency signal. In Morse code.* The signal that ships always send when they're sinking. So I tried it. Three short honks, three long honks, three short honks, over and over again. Surely somebody out there knew Morse code! Hadn't anybody seen *Titanic*?

I looked through the windscreen. I could see lights coming on in some of the apartment blocks, one or two lights at first, then more and more.

"Looks like we've woken the neighbours!" I cheered.

"VERY CLEVER!" yelled the Memory Man, suddenly appearing beside me. "GIVE ME THE KEYS... NOW!"

Somehow he always managed to beat us! One

minute he'd been outside banging on the door, the next he was inside grabbing my hand. *How did he do that?*

"THE KEYS, EUGENE!" he demanded, twisting my hand until I screamed with pain.

I dug out the keys and he swiped them away with a crooked smile. "At last! There's still time to get the money," he boasted. "But as for you three, you won't get away this time!"

He snapped his fingers. The biggest, longest, meanest looking python I'd ever seen was coiling itself down the aisle of the bus.

Samantha jumped onto a seat.

I froze, my sweaty hands clutching the steering wheel until my knuckles turned white.

But Azizul just laughed.

"Ha, ha, ha, Memory Man!" he mocked. He grabbed the python's tail. "You think you can fool us with your stupid snakes?" He waved the python's tail in the air, while the rest of the snake twisted around to attack him. Azizul roared with laughter. "This isn't a real python! *It's just the strap from Eugene's schoolbag!*"

I stared in horror. "Er, Azizul," I began, in a very quiet voice, "I... er... I think you'd better look over there behind you..."

Azizul turned to where I was pointing.

There, on the floor, half hidden under a seat, was the green plastic strap from my schoolbag.

Azizul looked at it, puzzled.

Then he looked at the massive, twisting thing he held in his hands.

And then his eyes rolled up until we couldn't see them any more.

And then he fainted.

Right on top of the writhing, wriggling python!

14
MUM

Everyone started yelling at once. Samantha was screaming at Azizul to get up. The Memory Man was shouting at me to open the door. And I was calling for someone to help us.

Then it all got even noisier!

Police sirens were wailing outside. Policemen were pounding on the door. The Memory Man was muttering strange words, trying to make himself disappear. What would Mel Gibson do now? Easy! I just flicked the lever and the bus door hissed open.

The police jumped on board. The officer-in-charge was shouting at everyone to be quiet.

"What's going on here?" he boomed.

The Memory Man dived for the door. He was pointing at us and yelling. "Stop those kids! They tried to steal my bus!"

Then Mr Ho was on board. He was yelling, too. "Stop that man! He tried to rob my bank!"

But the loudest of all was Samantha. She was screaming. *"Stop that python! It's trying to eat*

Azizul!"

The police rushed over to the snake. They lifted Azizul out of the way and chased the snake to the back of the bus. Another policeman grabbed hold of Samantha, lifting her clear over the seats and carrying her outside. I squeezed out from the driver's seat and ran down the steps.

Outside, I couldn't believe my eyes. Police cars blocked the street, their lights flashing blue and red. Hundreds of people in their pyjamas were crowded around to see what all the fuss was about. Newspaper reporters raced towards me. Their cameras popped in my face. Then a television van pulled up. More cameras spilled out, with cables *snaking* everywhere... yuk!

I searched the crowd. There were only two people I wanted to see. *And there they were!* Mum and Dad, standing to one side, dazed and worried. I ran towards them, waving my arms.

"It's all okay! We're safe! We stopped the Memory Man!"

Dad knelt down beside me. "Eugene, I want to know what's been going on..."

Poor Dad! He looked so confused! "Please," I begged him, "I want to go home..."

But we couldn't. Not yet. First, we were driven down to the police station. Samantha, Azizul and I were questioned by the detectives. Our parents just listened, open-mouthed.

"So, the driver's head *fell off*?" One of the policemen asked me, shaking his own in disbelief. "And then it *talked*?"

"And the bus drove *inside a tree*?" another one questioned me.

"And there was a *python* in your bedroom?" a third one wanted to be sure.

"Yes, yes, yes…" I groaned.

"You d-d-don't believe us?" asked Azizul.

"It all happened," sighed Samantha. "Really it did…"

One of the policemen stopped laughing and gave us a very serious look. "You *think* all those things happened, but really they didn't. You see, we've been trying to catch this Memory Man for a long time. He's more than just an illusionist," he explained, "he's also a *hypnotist*. He can look into your eyes and hypnotise you, he can make you see things and hear things that really aren't there. That's what makes him so *dangerous*."

"But what about the chicken-killer?" Azizul wondered. "And fish man?"

The police laughed. "Chicken-killer? You mean Albert, with the orange hair?" one of the detectives grinned. "We picked him up an hour ago. And Aloysius the fish seller has been arrested, too. So you don't have to worry about them, either."

Mr Ho cleared his throat. "Excuse me, officer," he began, talking to the senior detective, "if Eugene hadn't shown such bravery and taken my keys before the criminals got them, I don't know *what* would have happened. He and Azizul have both been very resourceful in stopping a crime."

The senior policeman agreed. "Rest assured, we *won't* forget to thank them…"

And they didn't! A few weeks later, the police came to our school assembly and presented Azizul and I with special medals. They called us heroes! You should have heard all the cheers we got. And then Samantha Ho had to go and spoil it! That afternoon, she kissed me in front of all her girl friends at the bus stop and I didn't know where to hide my red face…

So, you may think that "888" is still a lucky number after all? Don't you believe it. The Memory Man and his cronies may be locked up in gaol, but some nights I can *still* hear that evil wind howling in my bedroom, and the python *still* drops down from my ceiling now and then.

But one thing we did learn was how to use our memories. In fact, we've got very good at it.

So good, in fact, that Azizul and I can now turn ourselves into each other.

Like yesterday…

I can't play soccer for nuts. So Azizul took my place. He became me. And he kicked the winning goal. Which everybody thought I'd kicked!

And while he did that for me, I went over to his uncle's place and ate lots of *rendang*!

Scary, isn't it?

presents

REVENGE OF THE GOLDFISH

1
MUM

"Yes," I boasted to my friend Tik Koon, "my father has bought me a special goldfish. Do you want to know what's special about it?" I asked him.

Tik Koon sucked on his straw in the school canteen. He looked very *un*impressed.

So I whispered the secret.

"It has *no bones!*"

Tik Koon just stared at me. I think he thought I was mad. "All fish have bones!" He made this loud sucking noise on his straw. "If it doesn't have bones, what does it have? It's got to have something to hold it together."

"It's true!" I was getting angry. Tik Koon was my best friend. He *had* to believe me! "Dad told me it doesn't have bones."

Tik Koon shrugged. "You cannot have fish with no bones."

"But the man at the shop said so," I insisted. "He said it was a rare kind of goldfish that didn't have them."

"Not even little ones?" Tik Koon laughed.

"Not even one!"

"But how do you know?" snorted Tik Koon. "Did you X-ray it?" Then he giggled. "Maybe you should cut it open, then see if it's got bones or not," he suggested, squashing his drink carton.

I felt disappointed. "Well, you'll see it for yourself on Friday night when you sleep over at my place," I promised. "It's in my fishbowl."

"Tan Tik Koon! Bryan Lim! Didn't you hear the bell?"

We jumped. It was our teacher, standing right behind us, hands on hips, looking very fierce.

"You should have been on your way to class already," she scolded, as we scrambled to collect our bags. "What were you two talking about?"

"Goldfish," grinned Tik Koon. "Goldfish with no bones!"

"What sort of nonsense will you come up with next?" she demanded.

"But I've got one!" I told her.

"Stop talking," she warned, "and start moving!"

See? Not even my teacher would believe me.

That afternoon, when I got home from school, I ran straight to my bedroom. The fishbowl was where it always was, sitting on the shelf near my wardrobe. I went across and peered inside. Everything looked normal, just the way it should be. I had three old goldfish and one new goldfish. I stared at the new one. It didn't seem any different from the other goldfish, a bit more golden perhaps, kind of shiny. Except I knew that it didn't have any bones. *Unless the man at the shop had bluffed us!*

I unpacked my bag and started doing my homework. And that's when it started. A weird kind of feeling. Like I was being watched. I looked around my room. I was alone. There was just me, and the four goldfish.

I shook my head and went back to my maths. Then suddenly, I had this cold, shivery feeling on the back of my neck. I touched my skin. It felt wet!

I swung around in my chair, looking straight at the fishbowl. I gasped. All the goldfish were swimming around. Except one. *The new one.* It was just floating there, looking at me.

Bryan, I told myself, you're imagining things!

But a few minutes later, when I swung around in my chair, my new goldfish was *still* watching me, its goldfish face pressed up against the glass.

"Hey, mind your own business!" I shouted at it, and turned back to my books.

But it kept happening. Every time I looked at the fishbowl, my new goldfish was looking at me. It was all wrong! Goldfish weren't supposed to watch people. People were supposed to watch goldfish, right?

So when Mum called me for dinner, I was glad to get out of there.

We sat at the table, Dad and Mum, me and my sister Jasmine. Jasmine is twelve, two years older than me, and she never lets me forget it. *She* is older, so *she* is smarter, *she* gives the orders, you know what I mean. That night she was doing all the talking, too. Not that I paid any attention. I was too busy thinking about my new goldfish. Suddenly, when Jasmine stopped talking for a minute, I heard myself ask:

"Are you sure, Dad?"

Everyone looked at me.

"Sure about what?" Dad asked, looking puzzled.

"That new goldfish you bought me," I explained. "Everybody says all fish have bones. So how come my goldfish doesn't have any?"

"Oh…" Dad winked at Mum and she smiled. "Well, that's what the man told me. He said it was very special."

"It sounds fishy to me," Jasmine said through a mouthful of noodles.

"It's kind of… well, *strange*," I started to say.

"What, you? Or the fish?" Jasmine teased.

"The fish!" I retorted. "It kind of… well… *watches* me."

Jasmine rolled her eyes. "Next thing you'll say it can talk!"

"Well maybe it will one day!" I argued back.

Dad shot us a warning look. "That's enough!" He chose another piece of beef and some ginger. "You'll just have to watch the fish, Bryan, and see what it does."

"It keeps staring at me," I went on.

But Dad changed the subject and started talking about getting the car repaired. Adults are very good at changing the subject when they don't want to hear something. So *unfair*!

After dinner I went back to my room to finish my homework. And guess what? That goldfish was still looking at me with its beady little eyes. Every time I turned around, there it was, looking, looking, looking. I don't think it ever took its eyes off me!

So I took Dad's advice. I went over to the bowl and started to watch the fish. The more it looked at me, the more I looked at it. Maybe Tik Koon was right. Maybe it did have bones. Maybe I should take it out of the bowl and chop it in half! But, no, I couldn't, that would be wrong. And then, the more I watched it, the more it started to do strange things.

Like, the way it *moved*.

It was *faster* than the other goldfish.

So maybe Dad was right after all. It didn't have bones, so it was lighter, so it moved faster. That made sense, didn't it?

And when it did move, it swam differently. Most fish wiggle through the water, bending their tails and flapping their fins. But the new goldfish didn't. It almost *jumped* from one place to another, like it was trying to walk.

And then I noticed something else.

It wasn't just an ordinary goldfish. The other

goldfish swam at the top of the bowl, while the new goldfish stayed at the bottom. It was almost like the other goldfish knew that it *wasn't* the same as them!

When it came time to go to sleep, I got into bed and turned off my light.

And I still *knew* I was being watched, even in the dark!

I looked out from under the covers.

And saw these two little gold lights.

The fish's eyes!

They were glowing in the dark.

I pulled the covers over my head and tried to sleep.

And once, when I just *had* to have another look, there they were...

The two little gold lights!

The goldfish was still watching me...

And I began to wonder why.

Why...?

What did it *want*?

What was it going to *do*...?

2
MUM

In the morning I stumbled out of bed and whacked my alarm clock with a pillow. PLONK! That always stopped it ringing. For a moment I stood there, trying to wake up, and wondering why I felt so weird.

Like, *chilly.*

On the back of my neck.

I put my hand behind my head and rubbed my skin.

It felt damp.

No, not damp.

WET!

And then I remembered the goldfish, and the two little gold lights, and I shivered.

And that was when I *knew* something had happened in my room while I was asleep.

I took a deep, deep breath.

And turned, very, very slowly.

Very, very, very slowly.

And screamed!

Something had happened in my fishbowl.

Something that made all the little hairs stand up on my arms.

Yeeeeeeesh!

The fishbowl was still there, but now it was full! Full of just *one*, huge fish.

Yes, that's how big my new goldfish had grown!

It filled the *whole* bowl, and its eyes were as big as coins, and they just stared at me.

My door flew open and Mum ran in.

"Bryan, what is it?" she asked.

She saw my face. I must have looked really pale.

"Do you feel ill?" she wanted to know. "Do you need a *doctor*?"

I just shook my head and pointed at the fishbowl.

Mum frowned and turned around.

She gasped. Her voice sounded really shocked. "Oh! It's grown so fast..." Suddenly her tone was sad. "I wonder what happened to your other little fish?"

And just then, we saw them. All squashed up in a huddle behind the new goldfish.

"Oh dear," moaned Mum, "the poor little things. There's no room for them." She squeezed my shoulder. "Don't worry, dear, I'll put them in your father's fish tank in the lounge room. And your new goldfish can have this bowl all to himself..."

No, no, no! That was the last thing I wanted! Please, Mum, I thought to myself, don't leave me alone with that horrible fishy monster that can see in the dark!

But I couldn't just tell her that, could I?

"M-m-mum," I began, "maybe you should put the *new* goldfish in Dad's tank. Then it will have more room," I suggested.

Mum shook her head. "No, Bryan. What would your father think? He spent a lot of money buying you that new fish. He'd be very upset if you didn't want it…"

"I suppose so…" I mumbled.

Maybe I could find some other way to get rid of it, I hoped. Maybe Tik Koon could help me think of something!

And that cheered me up. Tik Koon would be sleeping over on Friday night. And that was tomorrow night! *That meant I'd only have one more night alone with that horrible fishy freak!*

While I had my shower, mum scooped out my little goldfish and took them into the lounge room. When I got back to my room, the new goldfish was waiting for me. Its big, bulging eyes watched me the whole time I got dressed.

"Don't you know it's rude to stare?" I asked it.

Its mouth opened and some big bubbles came out.

"And it's rude to answer back, too!" I added.

Its mouth opened again, and another burst of bubbles rose to the surface.

"You think you're so smart!" I snarled at it.

"Well, fishface, Tik Koon and I will fix you on Friday!"

More bubbles.

"And you, too!" I pulled a face.

My door swung open, and Jasmine looked in.

"Who are you talking to, Bryan?" she laughed. "Surely not your stupid fish?"

I pulled a face at her, too.

But Jasmine was too busy looking at the fishbowl.

"How gross!" she shivered. "It's got so fat and — and ugly!" Her mouth turned down in disgust. "How can you stay in the same room with that — that *thing*?"

Jasmine turned on her heel and walked out.

And the fish — well, it watched her go.

And as it did, its eyes became almost *human*.

There was a look in them I had never seen before.

A mean, angry look.

Really mean.

And *really* angry.

And its mouth curled back, like it was saying something, and a whole cloud of bubbles blew out.

Then it seemed to jump, and water sloshed over the top of the bowl.

For a horrible moment I thought it was going to *attack* us.

"Jasmine!" I yelled, and grabbed my schoolbag and raced from the room.

3
MUM

Tik Koon just laughed and laughed. "How could a fish grow *that* big in one night?"

"But it did!" I protested. "Mum saw it, too. And so did Jasmine!"

"Maybe the fish will want your whole bedroom," Tik Koon grinned, "and you'll have to sleep in the fishbowl!"

"Just wait! You'll see it tomorrow night!" I told him angrily. "Then you won't laugh at me!"

But when I got home from school that day, Mum met me at the front door. She looked really odd.

"Something funny has happened," she began, leading me into my bedroom.

We both stared at the fishbowl.

It was *empty.*

Well, almost.

A small goldfish was swimming around, not even looking at us, just minding its own business.

"It *shraaank!*" I moaned.

But the minute Mum left the room, the fish

changed.

It leapt up in the water, and pushed its face against the glass, and stared at me again, blowing hideous bubbles at me.

I backed away.

"W-w-what do you want?" I whispered.

The fish's mouth opened. More bubbles burst out. And its eyes had a strange, smug, cunning look.

I had to do something! I ran across to my desk. Mum kept some pieces of coloured board behind it for my school projects. I grabbed a small sheet and took it over to the shelf. I rested it against the fish-bowl. It was just the right size!

"Now I can't see you," I told the goldfish, "and you can't see me!"

I settled down to my homework. Once or twice I thought I heard a kind of *bubbling* sound, but when I looked around, the piece of board was still in place and the goldfish was safely out of sight.

But when I came back from dinner, I froze. The piece of board was on the floor, with wet sploshes all over it, and the goldfish was once again staring at me. It seemed to be *gloating*!

And when I went to bed, the two little gold lights were gleaming at me from the fishbowl. I fell into a deep dream about being a fish with a shark chasing me.

In the morning, when I hurled my pillow at the alarm clock, I shot a sleepy look at the fishbowl.

The goldfish had grown bigger again. And not just bigger, but *uglier*! Its eyes were like saucers, and its golden skin looked like metal. It was shining, like a big, hideous, golden bullet.

So I went over to the fishbowl and put on the toughest voice I could think of.

"Hey, you," I started.

The big, round, fishy eyes just blinked at me.

"You think you're so clever, right? Well, me and my friend Tik Koon are going to deal with you tonight…"

The goldfish eyed me with a menacing look. Then its mouth snarled open.

Bubble, bubble, bubble, bubble!

And that's when I began to tremble.

That goldfish was smart, really smart!

I just hoped that Tik Koon and I could handle it.

Because if we couldn't, I had no idea *what* might happen!

4
MUM

When I got home from school that afternoon with Tik Koon, the first person we met was Jasmine. And with her was her friend Sarah. Sarah was the same age as Jasmine. She wore these big, round glasses that made her look like a professor or something. But when she took them off, Tik Koon and I thought she looked like a movie star!

"Sarah's staying over, too," Jasmine announced, "and we've just been in to see your fish!"

Jasmine looked at Sarah, and Sarah looked at Jasmine. They burst out laughing.

"What's so funny?" I demanded. I could feel my cheeks burning.

"It's just an ordinary goldfish," Sarah said with a giggle.

"Has it got bones or not?" Tik Koon wanted to know.

"I think the man at the shop bluffed you," Jasmine said in her I-know-more-than-you-know voice. "Unless he took them out first then stitched it up again…"

She and Sarah ran off to her room, giggling and laughing with each other.

Tik Koon threw me a disappointed glance. "Your fish isn't big any more?"

I didn't know what to say, so I led the way to my bedroom. I opened the door and peered in. Everything looked normal. Even the goldfish. It was just swimming around in the bowl.

Tik Koon pushed past. *"Let me see, let me see…"*

Then he stopped and shook his head with dismay. "Sarah's right," he uttered glumly, "it's just a goldfish, but nothing special."

I tried to save my pride. "Right now it is, but you wait," I said, but even *my* voice sounded doubtful. Could I have imagined everything, I wondered. *But no!* Mum had seen it, and so had Jasmine. Everyone was just trying to make me look foolish!

Tik Koon and I listened to the radio and played some games until dinner. We didn't talk about the silly goldfish again. When we got back to my room, Mum came in with a folding bed for Tik Koon. We helped her set it up.

"If you need another pillow, Bryan knows where to get it," she told him.

We turned off the light and kept talking for a while. I was feeling very sleepy and my eyes were closing when suddenly Tik Koon gave a shout.

"Wow!" He reached over and nudged me. "Bryan, look!"

I was so tired that I'd forgotten all about the goldfish. But now I was wide awake again. *There, glowing in the dark, were the two little gold lights!*

"It can see in the dark!" Tik Koon was shaking with excitement. He leapt up and switched on the light.

And gave a horrified gasp!

"Bryan, look! It's bigger!"

He was right. The goldfish had grown a few inches longer, a few inches wider, and its eyes were the size of marbles. Angry-looking golden marbles!

And that was when Tik Koon had his Big Idea.

He turned off the light and started counting.

"One, two, three…"

"Tik Koon, what are you doing?" I asked.

"Four, five, six…"

And he kept counting, all the way up to…

"Fifty-eight, fifty-nine, sixty, one minute!"

And then he flipped on the light.

We both gasped.

In just a minute, the fish had grown even more. Its tail was the size of a ping-pong bat. Its eyes bulged like golf balls.

"Did you see that?" Tik Koon stared in amazement. "Your fish not only glows in the dark," he said, "it *grows* in the dark!"

"Wh-wh-what do you think we should do?" I asked through chattering teeth.

Tik Koon eyed the monstrous gold hulk in the fishbowl.

"B-B-Bryan…" he whispered, "m-m-maybe we should tell somebody…"

"Let's see if the girls are awake," I whispered.

But the girls had heard us already. There was a tap on my door and Jasmine crept in, followed by Sarah.

"What's all the noise about?" Jasmine started to say, then froze. For once, my know-all sister was lost for words!

"Oh no…" Sarah breathed, staring at the big, bloated goldfish.

"You haven't seen anything yet! Watch this," commanded Tik Koon, like a famous scientist about to conduct an experiment.

And with that he flicked off the light. The room was plunged into darkness, except for the two golden lights glowing in the bowl.

The two girls gasped in shock.

"Fifty-eight, fifty-nine, sixty…" I counted calmly.

Tik Koon flashed on the light and we all jumped with horror.

THE GOLDFISH HAD ALMOST *DOUBLED* IN SIZE!

Its golden eyes were like plates, its body was as thick as a hand, and its fins were the size of a schoolbook.

"It not only glows in the dark," said Professor Tik Koon, "it grows in the dark!"

"Scary!" gulped Jasmine.

But Sarah calmly took off her glasses and polished them on her pyjama shirt. "No," she announced, "there has to be a scientific explanation. Do you have an encyclopaedia?" she asked Jasmine. "We need more information…"

I looked at Tik Koon, and Tik Koon looked at me. And we both looked at Sarah.

"Just what we were thinking," I said.

And to show how clever I was, I walked over to the fishbowl and eyeballed the goldfish.

"Don't go away," I told it, "you may think you can scare us, but we'll fix you!"

There was a horrible bubbling sound and water splashed out of the bowl, up into the air and all down my pyjamas.

We raced from the room in terror.

5
MUM

It was midnight. We were crowded into Jasmine's room, searching through encyclopaedias and books for anything we could learn about my goldfish. Mum and Dad were asleep. We'd heard the television being turned off in their room.

"There's nothing in this book," yawned Jasmine.

"Nothing in this one either," moaned Tik Koon.

Sarah closed the big encyclopaedia which she had been reading. "Same here," she sighed. "Nothing at all about fish that have no bones, or fish whose eyes light up in the dark…" She looked very studious. She got up and started to pace around the room. "In my opinion, it is a rare fish. *And I have a theory…*"

We all stared at her.

"I think it must be a fish that lives deep in the ocean," she continued. "So deep, that there's never any light." She snapped her fingers. "Don't you see? When your fish becomes exposed to light, Bryan, it becomes smaller. But when you leave it in the dark, it grows back to its normal size."

"S-s-so if we left it in the dark even *longer*, then one night..." I swallowed with fear.

"Wow..." gasped Tik Koon. "You mean, it might grow two metres long, or ten metres..." His eyes bulged with horror.

"How gross!" Jasmine shuddered. Then she looked really alarmed. "What if the shop has more of those fish for sale? Maybe there are dozens of them... *hundreds* of them..."

Sarah's voice was very serious. "That's why we have to do something! We have to get *help*!"

I glanced at my watch. "But it's midnight..."

"Should we call the police?" Tik Koon wondered.

"What could they do?" Jasmine snorted. "They can't arrest a fish."

Suddenly Sarah stopped pacing. She pointed to Jasmine's computer.

"*We can surf the Net*," she suggested. "Maybe we'll find some answers there..."

A few minutes later we were huddled around the computer. We checked all the aquarium websites. Nothing! Then we checked the museums. Nothing there either!

"I know!" Sarah exclaimed.

She tried www.goldfish.com, then www.rare-fish.com. Still there was nothing!

So we started surfing as many websites as we could think of...

"www.seamonsters.com"

"www.deepsea.com"

"www.weirdfish.com"

"www.fishfacts.com"

Nothing, nothing, nothing, nothing! It seemed like we were the only people in the world who knew the secret of my goldfish.

So we kept trying again and again..

"www.fisheyes.com"

"www.nobones.com"

"www.fillet.com"

Then I had a thought. "What if... what if it's a *stolen* fish...?" So we tried "www.lostfish.com" and "www.missingfish.com", but still we had no luck!

By two o'clock we were all exhausted. We shut down the computer and sat in gloomy silence.

"Let's go back to bed," Tik Koon yawned.

"B-b-back in — *in there*?" I stammered. Suddenly I was shivering with fear.

"You can't stay in here!" Jasmine said firmly.

"W-w-we can leave the light on," Tik Koon considered. "then your fish won't get any bigger."

That made sense, even though it *didn't* make me feel any better. But we had no choice. Reluctantly I got to my feet.

"We'll try to get some answers in the morning," Sarah reassured us. "And we'll go down and visit that shop where your Dad bought the fish," she promised.

Tik Koon and I returned to my bedroom. The light had been on the whole time. The goldfish was smaller. It still watched us, whatever we did, but it certainly didn't look like a mysterious sea monster!

"How to sleep with the light on?" I moaned.

Tik Koon had another Big Idea.

"I know," he grinned. "There's a power point over here by your wardrobe. So we can take that lamp from your desk and put it inside the wardrobe with the fishbowl! Get it? That way we can turn out the big light, but leave a light on with the fish in the wardrobe — so it doesn't grow bigger!"

"Great!" I slapped him on the back and we did a high five. "And we won't have to worry about his eyes glowing in the dark all night!"

But I think the fish heard us.

Because when Tik Koon picked up the fishbowl, the goldfish went *crazy*. It started to flip over wildly in the water. Its eyes glinted with hatred through a fury of bubbles. Then it was thrashing its tail and water sloshed everywhere.

"Help!" wailed Tik Koon, holding the fishbowl as tightly as he could, his eyes wide with terror, his pyjamas soaking wet.

"Don't drop it!" I warned.

TOO LATE!

Tik Koon was so scared, he couldn't take his eyes off the furious fish. It grew so enraged that the whole bowl began to rock. Tik Koon's hands were shaking as they tried to grip the slippery glass. Every step he took became a nightmare. Suddenly I saw my skateboard on the floor, right beneath his feet. But before I could shout, he was standing on it. The next minute he was sailing across the room towards my bed.

CRASH!

SPLASH!

He landed on top of me. Water spilled everywhere and the fishbowl smashed on the floor.

"The fish! The fish!" I called, struggling to sit up, wiping water from my eyes.

But it had vanished!

We looked in the soggy sheets.

We shook the soaking pillows.

We even dived under the bed.

It had disappeared without trace!

Or so we thought...

Suddenly we heard a strange flapping sound behind us.

A strange, wet, slapping, flapping sound.

We spun around and our screams froze in our throats.

It was the goldfish!

Only now it was two metres long, and standing up, and moving towards us, with an evil look on its hideous face as it made bubbling, gurgling noises.

The most terrifying thing had happened...

It was no longer a fish...

It was a fish PERSON!

6

There were strange fish-like legs where its tail had been. Its fins had become arms which flapped against its golden body. It gulped in air through its mouth and its eyes were wet balls of hatred.

"Keep away!" Tik Koon shrieked.

The fish person shook its head. It opened its mouth again and a deep, watery voice came out.

"You tried to lock me up," it accused him.

"Y-y-you can *talk*?" I gasped. "And *breathe*? Just like us…"

"Of course," the bubbling, gurgling voice sneered. "I am not a fish. I am a *mammal*."

I backed against the wall. I was shaking from head to toe. I tried to remember what we'd learned about mammals at school. "You l-l-look like a fish…" My words were strangled with fear.

"I am part fish, part human," the fish person explained. It raised a dripping arm and pointed it straight at me. "Once, I was like you. *All* human."

"W-w-what happened…?" Tik Koon was trembling beside me.

The creature flapped its arms, spraying us with water. "Have you ever heard of the famous Lost City of Atlantis?" it asked us.

I nodded. Tik Koon and I had read about it. But surely it was only a legend, a myth.

"Thousands of years ago, our city was buried beneath the sea," the fish person said. "Some of us survived. We had to learn to live under water. But in our bodies... and in our minds... *we were still human beings...*"

Tik Koon's eyes were popping with shock.

"Sarah was right!" he burst out. "She said you were from deep in the ocean!"

"I heard what she said." The fish person nodded. "She was *almost* right."

"How could you hear what she said?" I demanded. "You were in my room, in the fishbowl!"

The fish person laughed. "Don't be alarmed, Bryan, it's not magic. Over the centuries we developed a very strong sense of hearing. But only in water," he added. "Our ears are attuned to sounds hundreds of kilometres away, so we can detect the approach of *predators*."

Tik Koon shook his head in amazement. "*Why* do you look like a goldfish?" he asked.

"Our city Atlantis was very rich and powerful," the fish person recalled. "Our clothing was made from gold silk. Our armoured suits were solid gold. When we were trapped under the sea, we turned gold. It was quite natural, I suppose."

"Can you remember your name?" Tik Koon wondered.

"Of course. In Atlantis my name was Rex," the fish person told him proudly. "We used the same language as the Romans. Rex, in Latin, means king. I was the king's son."

I had to pinch myself to make sure I wasn't dreaming. Nobody would *ever* believe a goldfish had once been the son of the ruler of the Lost City of Atlantis!

"If all this is true," I began, "how could my Dad buy you from a shop?"

Rex the fish person shot me an angry look. "Because there was an earthquake under the sea. I was blown to the surface and caught in a fishing net. When they discovered me, a golden fish amongst all the ordinary fish, they placed me in water, they kept me alive. Then they made up stories about me, and sold me for a lot of money." Rex was shaking with rage. "Of course I have bones! I am half human! *And now I have to come back to claim what is mine as a king's son!*"

"But — h-h-how?" I stammered.

"Because I know where to find the *gold mines* of Atlantis," Rex shouted. "*More gold* than the world has ever dreamed about! With that gold I will have my own army, my own kingdom, I will rule the world which my father once ruled!"

"People will stop you," I started to say, but Rex

grabbed me with one of his fins.

"People are greedy for gold!" he hissed in my face. "They will do what I tell them! Nobody — NOBODY — will be able to stop me!"

I could feel his grip tightening around me. "Tik Koon!" I shouted. *"Run for your life!"*

But Rex's other fin slapped itself around Tik Koon. The more we struggled, the stronger the pressure became.

"Now that you know my secret, I have to ensure your silence," Rex snarled.

For a goldfish, his power was enormous. He lifted us both clear off the floor and carried us into the lounge room. His fins had clamped around our mouths, too, so we couldn't call for help. Where was he taking us? What was he going to do? I began to sweat. He said he wanted to silence us. Did that mean... *kill us?*

He stopped beside Dad's fish tank in the lounge room.

"Centuries ago, my people had to learn to live under water," he whispered, his eyes flashing with a mean gleam. "Now, my friends, it is *your* turn..."

He lifted us high above the water. He was crazy! Tik Koon and I would *never* fit into the fish tank! And even if we did, how could we *live* under water?

Rex let out a horrible, bubbling, screaming sound that chilled my blood. Suddenly my whole body was shaking and twisting. My skin felt weird, like it was no longer skin any more...

I looked down at myself. I had scales! So did Tik Koon! Rex was turning us into goldfish!

Suddenly he plunged us down…

Down…

Down…

SPLASH!

I was under the water!

I couldn't breathe!

Air, air, I had to get air!

I was going to drown, I knew it!

I tried to breathe! I flapped, I flipped, I gasped and gurgled!

And then everything went BLACK!

7
MOM

I was alive! I blinked. Everywhere I looked there was water. And goldfish. And little pebbles and rocks and bubbles. And the water tasted funny. Not that I drank it. I just breathed it. It ran into my gills, and I got some oxygen, and I flipped my tail, and swam on.

"*Blub blub blub blub blub*, Bryan!"

It was Tik Koon's voice. But I couldn't look around. I didn't have a neck any more. I had to swim in a funny little circle. And there he was!

I wanted to laugh. He looked so funny with his big eyes and fins and tail. And he wasn't really a goldfish. He was blue. His whole fishy body was covered with blue stripes. Wow! Just like his pyjamas had been!

"Hi, *blub blub blub blub*, Tik Koon!" I greeted him.

He swam up alongside me, a crazy grin on his fish face. "You're *blub blub blub* still wearing your *blub blub blub* pyjamas!" he announced through a burst of bubbles.

I caught a glimpse of my reflection in the glass wall of the tank. He was right. I was covered with pyjama stripes, too! Erk, it was bad enough being a fish. Why did I have to be a stupid-looking fish?

I shuddered. "What are we going to do?" I begged. "We're trapped in here! And no one will ever *blub blub blub* know!"

Tik Koon swam over to the wall. "Where's Rex?" he asked.

I shook my head and joined him. We stared out into the lounge room and saw it the way a fish would see it. All watery-looking. Suddenly I could hear something. Voices! But the room was empty. So Rex had been telling the truth. I could hear sounds that were a long way off. Wow! It was fantastic.

When the door opened, Mum came in followed by my angry father.

"They broke the fishbowl!" he was saying.

"I wonder where they are?" Mum frowned with worry.

"Hmph!" snorted Dad. "Probably gone to the market for breakfast!"

Wrong, Dad! We're here, in the fish tank!

"Dad! Dad!" I cried through the mass of bubbles. I slapped myself against the glass side of the tank so he would hear me. *Ouch!*

Mum walked towards us, with the little packet of fish food she always uses. Food! My fish tummy rumbled. I was starving. Mum walked right up to the tank and looked down into the water. I started swimming round and round to catch her attention. I started doing backflips and twists.

"The fish look hungry," she said. "Especially that *blue* one."

"Mum!" I shouted, opening my mouth as wide as I could. "Mum, it's me! *Blub blub blub* Bryan!"

GLOMP!

I swallowed a mouthful of fish food. Yuk! It was revolting! What do they put in that stuff?

"I hope they come back soon," Dad complained gruffly. "I'm going to give them a piece of my mind. They must have knocked over the bowl and lost that fish!"

Mum shook more fish food into the tank. "But the fish wasn't in their room, dear," she reminded him.

"It must have died," he shrugged. "I paid a lot of money for that fish!"

"But you shouldn't have told him that silly story," she chided.

"About the fish not having bones?" Dad laughed. "Who'd believe that?"

"Bryan did!" snapped Mum.

"It was only a joke," Dad protested, and they left the room, still arguing.

So, Dad had played a trick on me.

And then the fish had played a trick on us all!

Where was Rex, I wondered. Was he hiding

somewhere? Or had he gone off to conquer the world with all the gold from Atlantis and left us in the fish tank for ever and ever?

"Blaaaa!" Tik Koon spat out some fish food. "How can fish eat it? It's gross!"

"We've got to do something!" I said urgently, trying not to panic. "We can't *blub blub blub* stay in here like this!"

"But what?" Tik Koon spluttered and choked, as he accidentally swallowed more fish food.

And suddenly he had another of his ideas...

"I know!" he shouted, frothing up the water.

"I hope it's a better idea than your last one," I warned. "Look at all the trouble *that* got us into!"

Tik Koon swished his tail. "I've been thinking! This tank is full of pebbles, right? And some of them are bigger than others, right? So, we use the big ones, and we push them together, and we write a message, like H - E - L - P!"

I stared at him. I was bubbling with excitement.

"T.K., you're a genius!" I told him.

We got to work at once, darting in and out of the other fish which must have thought we were mad. I used my big, fat fishy lips to carry the larger pebbles across the tank to Tik Koon, and he dropped them into place with his big, fat fishy lips. It seemed to take hours. One stupid fish tried to stop me, so I flicked it with a fin as hard as I could.

Tik Koon swam along to inspect his work.

The pebbles spelled a word...

"H - E - P - T."

"No..." I groaned. "You can't spell help like that!"

He dived down to fix his mistake.

"Quick, *blub blub blub!*" I called. "Someone's coming!"

I swished down to help him. Bubbles and pebbles went flying in all directions. Just as the door opened, we finished!

It was Jasmine and Sarah!

If only we could catch their eye...

If only we could make them look into the tank...

If only they could see our message...

"Jasmine *blub blub blub!*" we shouted. "Sarah *blub blub blub!* HELP... HELP... GET US OUT OF HERE!"

8
MUM

Jasmine and Sarah looked worried. Jasmine threw herself into a chair. Her red T-shirt made her skin seem even more pale. Sarah paced up and down. Her bright yellow top turned gold when she stood in the sunlight from the window.

We *had* to get their attention!

"Where could they be?" Jasmine moaned, staring straight at the tank. "I wish Dad had never bought that dreadful fish. It's been nothing but trouble!"

Tik Koon and I started swimming in crazy circles, wiggling and waggling, but Jasmine didn't even notice us.

"They'll be back soon," Sarah said hopefully. She frowned. "I wonder how they broke the fishbowl? Maybe they've taken the fish somewhere?"

Jasmine was scowling at the tank. We tried zigging and zagging. Tik Koon even tried a headstand.

"That's funny," said Jasmine. "I thought Dad had only twelve fish."

Sarah looked at the tank. She started counting. "Fifteen... sixteen... *seventeen* fish."

Jasmine got up, shaking her head. "Doesn't make sense. Dad had twelve, then he put in three of Bryan's. That's fifteen. So where did the other two fish come from?"

She was peering in through the glass, just inches away.

"Jasmine! It's us!" we shouted, spurting bubbles into her face.

"I haven't seen those two before..." She giggled. "They look like they're wearing pyjamas!"

Sarah came over, too, studying us through her big glasses. "So *cute*," she said.

Tik Koon and I started doing every fish trick we could think of. I did the Super Goldfish Upside Down Belly Roll. Tik Koon did the Amazing Fish Spin & Twist Super Special Tail Flip.

"Aren't they clever?" Jasmine pointed at us.

Then I did the Double Dare Belly Flop and Tail Spin, while Tik Koon did the Michael Jackson Underwater Moondance.

"Oh, so *sweet*," Sarah giggled.

Girls! *Girls!* We were right under their noses and they still couldn't see us! We were so tired we sank to the bottom and just floated there. Suddenly I knew we were going to spend the rest of our lives in a lousy fish tank!

"Jasmine! Look!" Sarah squealed, her eyes wide with shock.

She was pointing to the pebbles.

Jasmine saw them, too.

"HELP?" she said. "How did that get there?"

"Well, somebody wrote it," Sarah considered.

"But not the fish," Jasmine argued.

Sarah looked from the pebbles to us. When she spoke, her voice sounded really odd. "Jasmine, I've just had the *scariest* thought."

"What?" Jasmine wanted to know.

"I think the boys wrote it."

Jasmine nodded. "Yes, before they went out."

Sarah shook her head slowly. "No. They wrote it from *inside* the tank!"

Jasmine stared at her in disbelief. Then she laughed. "Sarah, stop trying to frighten me!"

Sarah leaned over closer. She tapped a finger on the glass.

"Bryan!" she called. "Tik Koon! It's you, isn't it? You're the two blue fish, aren't you?"

We swam over towards her and wagged our tails and fins as hard as we could.

"B-b-but how…?" Jasmine turned white. I thought she was going to faint. "H-h-how did you get in there?" she begged. "W-w-what happened to you?"

The girls were screaming and shouting so much, they didn't hear the door opening behind them.

But we did.

Because we were fish and we could hear for hundreds of kilometres!

And what we saw was REALLY scary.

Our eyes popped. Our fish bodies shook with fear.

IT WAS REX FROM ATLANTIS!

HE WAS CREEPING ACROSS THE ROOM!

HE WAS GOING TO GET THE GIRLS AND THERE WAS *NOTHING* WE COULD DO TO WARN THEM!

Rex the fish person moved closer and closer. His strong fishy fin arms were raised for the attack. We tried to bubble a warning.

"Jasmine! Sarah! *Blub blub blub!*" we shouted. "*BLUB BLUB BLUB!* LOOK OUT!"

But Jasmine just flashed us a nasty scowl. "What's the matter with them?" she asked Sarah. "You'd think they'd be happy to see us!" She poked out her tongue.

We waved our fins and we wiggled our tails. "YOU'RE IN TERRI*BUBBLE* DANGER!" I yelled. "*BLUB BLUB BLUB!*"

"Do you think they're trying to tell us something?" Sarah wondered, her glasses clacking against the tank.

Rex was right behind them, his eyes glittering with triumph.

"LOOK OUT!" gurgled Tik Koon, flapping his fins as hard as he could.

And then it happened!

Rex swooped in swiftly, seizing the girls with his fins, hauling them into the air.

"It's the goldfish!" screamed Jasmine, her face filled with horror, her legs dangling helplessly over the tank.

"You said I was *ugly*," Rex hissed at her in his watery deep voice. "You said I was *gross*! Well, what does it feel like now, being *CAUGHT BY A FISH*?"

"But y-y-you're not a fish!" Sarah spluttered, struggling against his fierce grip. "Let us go!" she demanded.

"Let you go?" Rex mocked her. "Certainly…"

He lifted them high above the tank, just like we had been, and made that same blood-chilling cry. Then he let them go and they dropped neatly into the water.

We watched in horror.

The girls stopped being girls.

They became fish.

Two little fish, one red and the other yellow, both with tails the colour of blue denim jeans.

"*Blub blub blub*," bubbled Jasmine the fish, waggling her fins and twisting her tail in shock. "I don't want to be a *blub blub blub* fish!" she sobbed.

Rex peered at her through the glass tank. "You should have thought of that before you were so rude to me!" he snarled.

"You can't leave us all here!" I begged.

"Too late!" Rex snapped, waving a fin to us as he

left the room. "I've got things to do. My kingdom will soon be mine again!"

The door slammed and we were alone. Alone in the tank, with no chance of *ever* getting out!

"Kingdom? What kingdom?" Sarah demanded, swishing around in the water. She still looked like a movie star. Well, a fishy one.

Tik Koon and I told the girls about Rex and the Lost City of Atlantis and the gold mines.

Sarah's eyes lit up. "If only we could stop him!" she sighed. "Rex is the most important scientific and historical discovery of the century," she said in awe.

Jasmine frothed the water with angry bubbles. "I don't care about science and history," she retorted hotly. "I want to go back to being ME!"

We all fell silent, and that was when Tik Koon said he'd had another Big Idea!

"Listen," he bubbled, "when your Mum and Dad turn off the lights, *blub blub blub*, we'll do what Rex did... we'll all grow bigger."

"And then?" Jasmine groaned.

"Well, the bigger we grow, the better," Tik Koon explained. "Then we'll be able to escape! We'll be so big, we'll be able to *climb* out of the tank by ourselves!" He looked at our astonished fish faces. "It's so simple," he added with a grin, "so what are we all worried about?"

"But don't you see," began Sarah, "if we do grow bigger, and if we do get out, we'll be *fish people*, just like Rex." She shuddered at the thought. "We'll have fish legs and fish arms *forever*!"

"I want my own arms back!" Jasmine demanded. "And my legs! I want to play tennis, and go swimming, and —" She swallowed. "No... I don't think I'll ever want to go swimming again..."

"That's for sure," I agreed.

How weird life was, I thought. Once I used to love swimming. Tik Koon and I used to go to the beach for hours. But when you're a fish, you see things differently.

And to make matters worse, if we were left in the dark, we'd all become fish people like Rex. I tried to imagine what I'd look like. Then I shut my eyes. I didn't want to know! We were trapped, and no one could help us now.

No one?

Well, there was still Mum and Dad. And just as I thought of them, the door opened and they walked in.

"MUM! DAD!" Jasmine and I yelled in a mass of froth and bubbles.

"MR LIM! MRS LIM!" chorused Sarah and Tik Koon.

But Mum and Dad were too busy talking to even notice us!

"Where could they be?" said Dad.

"Now the girls have gone, too," Mum fretted. "Why didn't they tell us where they were going?"

"Kids these days are terrible," complained Dad.

"WE'RE HERE!" we all spluttered, sending bubbles flying everywhere. "WE'RE *BLUB BLUB BLUB* HERE!"

"Maybe they've all gone to buy another goldfish," suggested Mum. "They're probably hoping you won't have found the broken bowl."

Dad's face brightened. "Well, let's go shopping." He looked at his watch. "It's almost lunchtime and I'm starving…"

And off they went.

Leaving the four of us floating in the tank, *without any hope of escape at all.*

10
MUM

The afternoon dragged on. With our fish hearing we could listen to the neighbour's TV, and the traffic outside, but nobody came home. Mum and Dad were taking their time! And the longer they took, the less chance we'd have of being found before it got dark. And once it was dark, I gulped, we'd all start to grow like Rex. We'd all become big, weird fish people *and that would be the end of us*!

It was four o'clock on that Saturday afternoon when I first heard the strange noise. I had been napping. Suddenly I was wide awake, listening to a flapping, slapping sound that was getting louder and louder. The others were straining to hear it, too. A wet kind of sound, like a huge jelly wobbling!

The door burst open. Rex staggered in, his golden skin covered with dust and grime. His eyes were wide with fear and he was gasping for breath. He lurched over to the tank and glared at us.

"I... *hate*... your... world..." he announced, sucking in air as fast as he could. "I am going back to Atlantis," he said, "where I... belong..."

Whatever could have happened to him? He was trembling all over, hanging on to the tank with his fins.

"All human beings are just like you," he accused us. "They *laughed* at me. They... they *chased* me... they threw things at me..." He lifted his head proudly. "When I told them I was the king's son, they... they *mocked* me..."

Sarah swam towards him. "People don't understand," she began. "You mustn't blame them."

"Your streets are full of horrible things that make smoke and noise," he wailed.

"Cars and buses," I told him.

"And there were blue soldiers who tried to catch me," he said in a frightened voice.

"The police," said Jasmine. "They must have wondered what you were..."

Tik Koon gave a sudden bubbling sound. "Rex, if you want to go back to Atlantis," he said, "you're going to need our help!"

"How can *you* help me?" Rex demanded.

"If you want to go home, you'll have to reach the sea," Tik Koon explained. "And we're the only ones who can show you where it is!"

It was another Big Idea from Tik Koon, but this time he was right! The fish person needed us, as much as we needed him.

Rex stared at us. "Why should I trust you?"

"Because we're the only ones who know who you

really are," I replied. "Without us, you'll *never* make it."

"So you *have* to let us out of here," Jasmine begged.

"So we can help you go home," added Sarah.

Rex looked down at his fish feet. "Do you mean it," he mumbled, "about helping me? After all I've done to you…"

"Of course we do," said Sarah. "We don't want to stay in this horrible tank any more than you want to stay in our world!" She shivered. "But you'll have to hurry. Once it gets dark we'll turn into fish people, too, and then it will be *too late!*"

Rex reached a fin into the tank and scooped up Sarah. He lifted her clear of the water with a screaming sound and shook her, spraying water everywhere. Suddenly she turned back into a human and was standing beside him.

"Quickly!" she cried. "Get the others out!"

Rex was dipping his fin into the water to pick up Jasmine when he froze.

We'd heard it, too. The front door.

Mum and Dad were back!

If they caught sight of Rex, for sure they'd call the police. And if anything happened to Rex, we could never return to being humans again.

"Hide! Hide!" I yelled to Rex and Sarah.

But the lounge room door was beginning to open already…

11
MUM

Sarah pushed Rex towards the couch. She pulled it out from the wall and he dived down behind it. She had no sooner flung herself onto the couch than Mum and Dad walked in.

"Sarah!" Mum gasped in a surprised voice.

"Hi, Mrs Lim!" Sarah said with a sweet smile as though nothing was wrong.

Dad looked around, sniffing. "Where's Jasmine? Where are the boys? And what's that funny *smell* in here?"

"They'll be back very soon," Sarah promised.

"Our car broke down," Mum explained. "That's why we've been gone so long. We had to get a tow truck."

"I can smell fish." Dad wrinkled his nose. He glanced at the tank. "Is it my imagination or is it getting *crowded* in there?"

He started to cross towards the tank but Sarah leapt up. "Er, Mr Lim," she called, "I, er, I think the boys are going to surprise you," she blurted.

Dad stopped and turned back. "Is that so...?" He looked at Mum and winked. "Well, I'd better not spoil it then."

He walked to the door.

Squelch, squelch.

He looked down.

"The carpet's all wet," he began.

"Oh, er..." Sarah nervously waved her hands about, trying to think of something to say. "It's all p-p-part of the surprise," she offered weakly.

Dad yawned. "I need a sleep before dinner..." He headed for the door.

Mum hesitated, then she followed. "I'd better start the cooking..." She lowered her voice. "Sarah, are you *sure* everything's all right?"

Sarah laughed happily. "Oh, everything's *fine*, Mrs Lim..."

The minute the door had closed, Sarah pulled Rex out from behind the couch. She dragged him, flapping and spluttering, to the tank.

"Hurry!" she urged. "Before something else happens..."

Rex reached into the tank and pulled us all out together. He shook us in the air, uttering his eerie screaming sound. As he did, I could feel my body stretching. My fins turned into arms, my tail became legs, and I was back to being a human again!

"Wow!" gasped Tik Koon. "What a cool trick!"

Jasmine glared at him. *"Cool?* You must be crazy!"

"Now what do we do?" Rex asked anxiously.

"We take you to the sea!" I promised. Then I stopped. "Er, one little problem," I announced, turning to the others. "How are we going to do that?"

Tik Koon just shrugged. "Easy. Catch a bus."

"But we can't take Rex on a bus!" I argued. "What will people say?"

Rex slumped onto the floor. "But you promised you'd help me go home…" He stared at us sadly. "You can't break your word! *Not now…*"

We looked at him, then at each other. I grabbed one of his fish arms.

"We won't let you down! Trust us!" I told him. "Don't worry… Tik Koon will have one of his Big Ideas!"

Tik Koon looked at me blankly. "I *will*?"

"You'd better!" Jasmine prodded him.

I opened the lounge room door and peered out. I could hear Dad snoring in his bedroom. And pots and pans were clanking in the kitchen. The coast was clear!

I waved for the others to follow me and crept across to the front door.

We made it safely to the corridor. We scuttled to the lift, Rex flapping and flustering along. At first, he refused to get in.

"We should go down the stairs," he protested, peering into the lift suspiciously.

"It's an elevator," Sarah explained. "It carries us

up and down without walking."

Rex was stunned. He looked around. "But where are the slaves to pull it?"

"No slaves, Rex," Jasmine told him, jabbing the button. "Electricity."

"I can see your world does have some advantages over Atlantis," Rex admitted.

When the doors opened on the ground floor, three old ladies took one look at us and started screaming.

Four kids with a walking, talking fish.

And Tik Koon and I were still in our pyjamas.

Very wet pyjamas...

But things got worse when the bus arrived.

As we started to climb on board, the passengers began to scream and shout.

"Hey!" yelled the driver. "You can't bring that — that *thing* on board my bus! And you can't ride on the bus in your pyjamas, either!"

We all turned to Tik Koon. It was time for his next Big Idea!

"Er... ah..." he stammered. Then suddenly an idea struck. He shot the driver a sheepish grin. "We're just dressed up for our school play!" he said.

The driver snorted. "I've never heard of any school play with a fish like that in it!"

"There is! What school did *you* go to? Haven't you heard of the story about the whale called *Moby Dick*?" Tik Koon asked indignantly. "We couldn't get a whale costume, so we took the fish one!"

"You mean, there's somebody *inside* that fish?" the driver gaped.

"Yes," announced Rex, in a deep, watery voice. "Me."

The driver was horrified. "Well, if it's your school work, you can come on board..." He glared at Rex. "But the fish pays adult fare!"

Sarah and Jasmine turned out their pockets. They had just enough to get us to the beach and back again.

We made our way to some seats at the back. Poor Rex was squashed between Jasmine and I. His long fishy legs poked out into the aisle.

"Not far now," I whispered.

He gave a frightened grunt.

Whew! We'd made it, I thought. Nothing could go wrong now! In a few more minutes we'd be at the beach and Rex could start his long swim home. I closed my eyes.

"MEOWWW!"

I thought I was dreaming.

"MEOOWWWWRRRRRR!"

My eyes popped open. My stomach was knotted with fear.

Across the aisle sat an old lady with a basket.

A cat basket.

And the lid was vibrating wildly.

"MEOWWWW! MEOWWWW! *MEOWW-WRRRRRRR!*"

The lid was being ripped to shreds.

Her cat had smelt a fish.

The biggest fish it had ever smelt in its life.

And now the cat was *VERY, VERY HUNGRY*!

12
MUM

I jumped up and grabbed the cat basket. The old lady screamed at me. The man sitting beside her yelled for me to stop.

"Cat thief!" he called.

Then everybody started shouting at once.

"Run for it," I told the others.

Rex was on his fish feet, wobbling down the aisle. The girls chased after him, while Tik Koon and I fought to keep the lid on the basket. Tik Koon made savage barking noises.

"How dare you steal that old lady's cat!" cried a woman.

"But I get sick when I go near cats!" Tik Koon told her. He started making hideous groaning and coughing sounds. His eyes were rolling everywhere.

The bus braked to a stop. The driver got out of his seat and came running towards us.

"No pets are allowed on my bus!" he yelled.

"Well you let that fish on board!" somebody

yelled back.

"There was somebody inside the fish!" the driver argued. "And the fish paid his fare!"

"I'm calling the police," shouted a man with a handphone.

"I'm getting off!" shrieked the lady with the cat. "I've never been so insulted in my life."

"No! Stay where you are!" I begged, pushing the basket towards her. "*We'll* get off!"

We were close enough to the beach anyhow, I guessed. Better we walked the rest of the way than have the police arrest Rex for insulting the cat lady.

We dashed for the door and hurried away. Sarah and Jasmine took the lead, helping the quivering, quaking Rex across the road. We followed.

I could see families having barbecues by the beach. Dogs were barking, too. *Oh no! We'd never make it!*

"This way!" Jasmine had found a path through the trees. It was dark and shadowy. Hopefully nobody would see our strange procession of two girls, two boys in their pyjamas — and a big, walking fish!

At last, we reached the water's edge. We stood there, panting for breath, looking out to sea. Rex turned to speak to us. One by one we shook his fin.

"It is time to say goodbye," he said sadly. "You have been very good friends to me."

"I wish you could have seen more of our world," said Sarah. "It's not such a bad place, really."

"We could have taken you to the movies," Jasmine smiled. "It's nice and dark in the movies, and no one would bother you."

Rex patted her shoulder. "No, I must return to my real kingdom."

"Will you know where to find Atlantis?" I asked him.

Rex took a step into the water. "I will follow the great currents. Have no fear for me. The water is my home…"

"Goodbye, Rex," waved Tik Koon.

Rex waded out further. Soon the water had almost covered him. He turned back one last time.

"What about your parents? How will you explain what happened?" he wanted to know.

"We'll think of something," I called.

"Will we ever see you again, Rex?" sobbed Sarah.

But he had gone, vanished beneath the water. We stood there, staring at the place where he had disappeared. And once, I'm sure of it, I saw the two little gold lights of his eyes as he swam in search of the right current.

13
MUM

It was dark when we got home. Dad was going to be furious with me, I just knew it. And not even Tik Koon had been able to think of what to tell him!

We staggered into the lounge room, exhausted, and Jasmine dropped into a chair.

Mum jumped up from the couch. "Where have you been?" she demanded. "You've been gone all day and now dinner is getting cold."

"It's a long story, Mum," Jasmine sighed.

I looked across at Dad, but he was down on his knees, staring into the fish tank.

I was lost for words. I thought Dad would have been really angry with us, but he was too busy gazing into the tank.

"Dad," I began nervously, "I'm sorry if you've been worried about us…"

"Bryan!" he called. "Come and look at this!"

I shared a startled glance with the others and walked across to join him.

Squelch, squelch. Wow! The carpet was really

wet!

"Look!" he pointed into the tank. "Look at those pebbles!"

"Yes?" I asked thinly.

"Well can't you see what they *say*?" he asked excitedly. "Someone has written the word HELP with pebbles in the fish tank!"

And that was when I had my first Big Idea!

"Oh that?" I laughed. "Dad, do you see that green fish at the back of the tank? It was him! We *taught* him how to do it!"

**COMING SOON!
IN BOOK #4**

presents

MY CREEPY COMPUTER

Here's a ghostly glimpse of
this new tale of terror...

1

"NO WAY I WILL SURRENDER!"

My name is Ashraf and I was playing X-Men with my smaller brother, Hafizuddin. I usually call him Hafiz. And I usually beat him. That's because I memorise all the special moves for all the characters and he doesn't know how to unleash even *one* special move!

"Not fair, not fair!" he scolded me, banging the table.

I laughed. So did my friend Ting Xuan from next door.

"Ashraf is sure to win!" TX chided him.

"He always does!" protested Hafiz, jabbing a finger at the computer. "This computer's no good!"

GRRRRRRRAWK!

We jumped. It was an odd sound, and it had come from the computer. Almost like the computer had answered him!

"What was that?" TX asked, staring at the monitor.

"I don't know…" I shook my head.

Suddenly the screen went funny. Funny, like strange, like weird. There were wavy lines all over it. And flashes. Bright flashes. And the characters went all wobbly.

"Told you," shouted Hafiz. "The computer is no good!"

QUAAAACKKK!

"What's happening?" I was on my feet. What was my computer doing? Why was it making all those weird noises?

Before I could do anything, the screen suddenly went blank. Totally blank!

"Quick," called TX. "Hit the reset key!"

I tried. I was just about to press it when the screen burst into life again. But our game had vanished. Instead, something else was forming on the screen. We froze, watching a word taking shape.

H…

"Wow! It's going to spell my name!" shouted Hafiz.

Wrong! The next letter came on in a blast of colour…

E…

"Has it ever gone like this before?" TX whispered.

I shook my head, my eyes glued to the computer. The next two letters zapped up to fill the screen…

L…

P…

"Help…" TX read aloud. "Help? Help who? Help what?"

"I don't know," I shrugged. "It's not part of the game, is it?"

"It doesn't make sense," puzzled TX.

"It must be a message," Hafiz said, his eyes glowing with excitement. "Somebody's trying to contact us!"

"Don't be silly," TX told him. "We're not on the Net or anything. *Nobody* can contact us!"

"But what if somebody was?" Hafiz demanded. "What if… what if it was coming from… *somewhere else*?"

"You've been watching too many movies!" TX sneered.

"I have not!" Hafiz tried to punch him.

"I think the computer must be spoiled," I argued. "I'd better tell Dad. He'll know what to do…"

TX stared at the word on the screen. "What if the computer is telling us it needs fixing. Maybe something's gone wrong inside."

"I think it's a message from somebody," insisted Hafiz. "They're asking us for help or something."

I ignored him. Sometimes, my brother's imagination drove me crazy! "I think we should turn it off, just in case," I said. "If the computer is spoiled we don't want to do any more damage."

So I shut it down and turned to face the others. "Done…"

But they weren't looking at me. Their eyes were

wide with horror.

"Ashraf…" TX whispered, "look…"

I swung back to the computer.

I gasped.

I couldn't believe my eyes.

It was impossible!

The computer was back on again.

I'd just shut it down, but it was still on.

And the word "HELP" was still on the screen.

Only now it was flashing on and off, on and off…

"HELP…"

"HELP…"

"HELP…"

"HELP…"

Hafiz grabbed my arm. "I told you, I told you," he screamed. "Somebody's sending us a message! What are we going to do…?"

2
MUM

Maybe Hafiz was right. Maybe someone, somewhere, *was* calling us for help. Or maybe we had just gone crazy!

"I'll tell you what we're going to do," I announced. "Nothing! Dad will be home from work soon. We'll ask him!"

TX couldn't take his eyes off the flashing screen. "It's just like a... a weird signal..." He rubbed his eyes.

"What if it's from someone in trouble?" Hafiz wondered. "Or someone on another planet? What if they have special powers, what if they want to invade us...?"

"What if the computer's just hung?" I retorted. I was really getting a headache from that silly flashing "HELP". *I* was the one who needed help! "Let's go and watch TV till Dad gets home," I suggested.

So we all trooped out of the bedroom and turned on the TV. Mum was cooking in the kitchen. She looked around the door.

"Who won?" she asked.

"No one," Hafiz cried. "But we got this weird message from Mars or somewhere!"

"Rubbish! We didn't!" I snapped.

Mum winked at me. "Maybe they were worried about all your homework," she joked, then went back to her cooking. Adults always find a way to nag about your homework, don't they?

"Maybe your computer *did* pick up a special message," TX whispered. "Some kind of radio waves, you know? Maybe the wires picked it up or something. Maybe the police can trace it, what do you think?"

I shot him an angry look. What was wrong with everyone? I was about to say something when I heard the front door open.

"It's Dad!" screamed Hafiz.

We all jumped up and rushed over. We all started talking at once. Hafiz began pulling him by the arm.

"Quick, quick," he yelled, "come and look what the computer's doing!"

Poor Dad, he didn't know what to do. Suddenly he looked really worried. "You haven't broken it already?" he asked.

"No, Uncle," TX shook his head. "But it's been picking up secret messages…"

Dad threw back his head and laughed. "Oh, well that's okay then…" He scratched his head. "I suppose I'd better see…"

Hafiz dragged him into the bedroom. TX and I squeezed in behind them. And we all stood there, staring…

Staring…

At the shut down computer with the blank screen!

"*Huh…?*" TX blinked.

"It's *tricked* us!" Hafiz shouted.

I explained to Dad what had happened, how the computer kept flashing a "HELP" message after I'd turned it off.

"Well, it's certainly turned off now…" He frowned. "Maybe there was a fault caused by the software. Let me know if it happens again and I'll get it checked."

"But, Dad, what if the message was real?" Hafiz argued. "What if someone was in trouble?"

"We'll be in trouble if we don't go and have dinner…" Dad grinned and ruffled his hair.

TX went home and we sat down to eat. Hafiz tried to talk about the computer, but Mum and Dad were soon too busy working out all the things they had to do on the weekend. Then it was time to do my homework. So much to do, my maths and my English. Hafiz was asleep already when I closed my last book and stuffed it into my bag for the morning.

I was yawning and my eyes were half-closed. As I got undressed, I kept looking at the computer.

What had really gone wrong, I wondered. Was it the X-Men game? I yawned again and fell into bed.

It was well after midnight when I suddenly woke up. It was a warm night, but I was shivering. I stared at the ceiling. Something had disturbed me, but what?

Everything seemed normal. I could hear Hafiz snoring. I could hear Mum's clock in the lounge room chiming. No, that wouldn't have woken me. So what could it have been?

My eyes were beginning to close when I heard it again! The softest sound, coming from the corner of the bedroom.

Click, clack… click, clack…

An insect? Something beating its wings? I sat up in bed and looked across the room into the darkness.

Only the darkness *wasn't* dark!

There was a square of light showing on my desk. The computer! The computer was on!

And on the screen was that message, flashing on and off again…

"HELP…"

"HELP…"

"HELP…"

"HELP…"

But this time it was worse… this time it wasn't just the message I could see… this time it was the mouse… the mouse was glowing… the mouse was alight… and it was almost too dazzling to look at!

It was bright red... like it was on fire!

And as I watched, it seemed to throb...

And vibrate...

And the red light was burning even hotter and brighter...

And it seemed to be moving...

Like it was... *ALIVE*!

A DOUBLE DARE FROM

MrMidnight

MrMidnight DARES YOU to write to him with the first page of any story you can think up. And he'll finish it! The stories that **MrMidnight** chooses will win the SCARIEST prizes, chosen personally by **MrMidnight** and Angsana Books.

MrMidnight DARES YOU to put your friends into the next **MrMidnight** stories. Tell him their names and he'll put them into terrifying danger! And **MrMidnight** will present you the WEIRDEST prize!

Send your entries to:

MrMidnight,
c/o Angsana Books,
Flame Of The Forest Pte Ltd,
Yishun Industrial Park A,
Blk 1003, #02-432,
Singapore 768745.